Hunter and the Quarry

"Steldan! Come out! We have a warrant for you! You won't be harmed! Surrender!"

Sweat flashed to Steldan's forehead. "Never!" he shouted, and with a shower of crumbling ceiling panels he crashed through to the glass-strewn carpet, knocking a security man to his knees, and himself rolling on shoulder and hip through the door. A second he lay numb; a second the soldiers stood shocked; then Steldan was on his feet, moving down the hallways at top speed.

He soon found himself in unfamiliar territory, among the lower rent offices. Ahead, two corridors intersected, offering him some choice. There were no witnesses. The Spaceport was like a small city, nestled within the confines of Leonidas City. Hiding places could be found, with a little ingenuity, that might require weeks of intensive search to be revealed. The Concordat had those weeks—although possibly not much more—and if Commodore Higgins or Admiral Horst ever caught him, death by ionization would be more kind . . .

Other Avon Books by
Jefferson P. Swycaffer

NOT IN OUR STARS

Coming Soon

THE UNIVERSAL PREY

Avon Books are available at special quantity discounts for bulk purchases for sales promotions, premiums, fund raising or educational use. Special books, or book excerpts, can also be created to fit specific needs.

For details write or telephone the office of the Director of Special Markets, Avon Books, Dept. FP, 1790 Broadway, New York, New York 10019, 212-399-1357. *IN CANADA:* Director of Special Sales, Avon Books of Canada, Suite 210, 2061 McCowan Rd., Scarborough, Ontario M1S 3Y6, 416-293-9404.

BECOME THE HUNTED

JEFFERSON P. SWYCAFFER

AVON
PUBLISHERS OF BARD, CAMELOT, DISCUS AND FLARE BOOKS

Several of the concepts and nomenclatures used in this story are from the games Imperium ™ and Traveller ®, published by Game Designers' Workshop and designed by Marc W. Miller, to whom all my thanks for his kind permission regarding this use.

—J.P.S.

BECOME THE HUNTED is an original publication of Avon Books. This work has never before appeared in book form. This work is a novel. Any similarity to actual persons or events is purely coincidental.

AVON BOOKS
A division of
The Hearst Corporation
1790 Broadway
New York, New York 10019

Copyright © 1985 by Jefferson P. Swycaffer
Published by arrangement with the author
Library of Congress Catalog Card Number: 84-091772
ISBN: 0-380-89608-7

All rights reserved, which includes the right to reproduce this book or portions thereof in any form whatsoever except as provided by the U. S. Copyright Law. For information address Ashley Grayson Literary Agency, 1342 Eighteenth Street, San Pedro, California 90732.

First Avon Printing, July 1985

AVON TRADEMARK REG. U. S. PAT. OFF. AND IN
OTHER COUNTRIES, MARCA REGISTRADA, HECHO EN
U. S. A.

Printed in the U. S. A.

WFH 10 9 8 7 6 5 4 3 2 1

This book is dedicated to Andrew J. Offutt, who, as an editor, bought my very first piece of professional fiction, and who, as a writer and a friend, has been helpful, insightful, inspiring, and kind. Thank you, Andy.

Due to the urgencies of the publishing schedule, this book, although following *Not In Our Stars* into print, takes place before that book in internal storyline time-sequence. Each book stands perfecty well on its own, however; neither is, strictly speaking, a sequel to the other.

                                     Jefferson P. Swycaffer,
                                     San Diego, 1985.

"I see a hare chase a hound
twenty miles above the ground . . ."
>   Thomas Ravenscroft,
>   "Who's the fool now?"

"Let the hunter become the hunted . . ."
>   Anon.

The Praesidium:

- Secretariat: First Secretary Parke (two votes)
- Judiciary: Justicar Solme
- Navy: Secretary Telford
- Treasury: Secretary Wallace
- Foreign Service: Secretary Vissenne
- Commerce: Secretary Redmond

The Navy:

Secretary of the Navy
Grand Admiral Telford
|
Chief of Naval Operations
Admiral Cambrai
|
Vice-Chief of Naval Operations
Admiral de la Noue
|
Chief of Naval Intelligence
Admiral Horst

Chief of Investigations   Chief of Intelligence Records
Commodore Higgins   Commodore Rudolfs
                                    |
                                    All-Sectors Coordinator
                                    Captain Athalos Steldan
Subsector Coordinator
Commander Finch

Lieutenant Ron Gray

Prologue

"If I were you, pal, I'd go to ground. Dig in. Bury yourself."

"But . . ."

"Don't thank me—clear out. I'm boosting in ninety seconds."

Athalos Steldan, exile, turned from the low-hovering spaceship that had brought him to the planet Chirkun, and ran. A chill wind whipped at his coat as he ploughed through tall waving grasses. As far as he could see in all directions, weeded hills bulked low and dark green beneath an overcast sky. The air was bitter, the sunlight hidden behind sailing masses of cloud cover. Running became painful; he felt the fiery bite of the wind. After an age, he heard the dull blast of the spaceship slamming into the air and upward, outward, away.

"Bastard . . ." he panted, and slowed to a steady jog. He dared not linger; the Chirkun Close Orbit Command by now had certainly pinpointed the illegal landing and takeoff. Satellite reconnaissance, Scout overflight, armed investigating teams would all be swooping low to investigate. Even now Steldan's body heat, radar image, or—*Bastard!* he cursed silently—trace radiation dosage from the takeoff could be showing on a dozen 'scopes.

He ran. Harried, hunted, he became the prey, and he ran. Catching his second wind, he settled into a long-distance lope.

"Dig in . . . dig in . . ." he breathed, crossing the endless green ocean of high grass. Digging in meant cities, people, the thousand bolt holes of civilization. It meant security patrols, checkpoints, and I.D. numbers as well, but these were things that Steldan knew well.

Athalos Steldan, tall, well-formed, with a wide, normally cheerful face and dark hair, with gray-green eyes and a quick wit, always left behind him the impression of being an honest man. Once he'd been an administrator, a physician, and an interrogator with Concordat Naval Intelligence. Now, the resources of an entire planet could be mobilized against him. He held hope that he would yet escape; he counted heavily on the slowness that all too often crippled government operations.

Imagining he heard the whine of Scout patrols overhead, he shifted course and ran on. Far ahead in the fading afternoon he saw the black line of a road. He ran toward it.

Part I
Months of Seeking

Brantos, Brantos, and Bourtzos, shipping brokers, occupied a lavish office suite on the second floor of the Spaceport Annex. In the plush interior, decorated in a soft pastel blue behind blue glass doors, John Bourtzos oversaw the operations of five well-trained clerks. Short and dark, Bourtzos greeted all customers—"Clients, Patrons, Partners in interstellar commerce"—with the same molded, unvarying smile. From the lowest freight jockey to the vice president of BirkenLines, everyone who dealt with him received the identical insincere grin.

That grin had faded only twice, and both occasions were permanently engraved upon the memory of every clerk in the firm as events of the highest possible embarrassment: when one drafts clerk had been caught embezzling, and when a space pilot had attempted to enlist the firm of Brantos, Brantos, and Bourtzos as backers in a smuggling adventure.

Scorning the illegal in favor of the merely ruthless, the firm stood steadfastly on the right side of the law; Bourtzos would have it no other way.

Today, he brushed past his senior clerk, L. Tempes, on his way to the reception area. "Stand by," was all he said, and Tempes only nodded. The relations between the two were dour at their very best.

Leaving his cubicle and heading for the inventory atlas, Tempes saw Bourtzos speaking to a stranger in the lobby. Unobtrusively, Tempes moved to watch the meeting from the doorway. Bourtzos evidently wished to have his clerk present, yet unseen, during this transaction, to double-check whatever offers might be made, or to be handy in case a document needed to be witnessed.

Tempes saw a youngish, slightly disheveled man, hatless, dripping rainwater onto the thick blue carpet. The gentleman's visage impressed Tempes despite the not-quite-appropriate attire. The trouser knees had recently been scraped of mud—quite thoroughly. Few others than Tempes would have noticed. He listened carefully, aware that Bourtzos was now aware of him.

". . . Quite a bit of experience with operations of this kind, sir," said the damp stranger. "For a time I was with the Commerce Department, as a . . . junior clerk." For a year and a half, Athalos Steldan had been a sector-level third Under Secretary of Commerce. That was before he'd been commissioned into the Navy, a move that had led him here, running for his life.

Bourtzos pretended not to notice the hesitation, although Tempes, watching from his casual concealment, knew that his employer *had* taken notice.

"We have set for ourselves very exacting standards, Mr. Tiernif," Bourtzos said, referring obliquely to Steldan's clothing. His plastic smile disfigured his secretive face. Tempes heard the subtle acid in the voice, and refrained from wincing sympathetically. *Bend and withdraw, fool,* he subvocalized. Not hearing this silent advice, Steldan, alias Ramo Tiernif, pressed his case.

"I agree I'm not dressed very well; I'm far from home, and from my days of expensive suits. However, if you would be so kind as to glance at my references"—he did not add *forged*—"you may find that I have something to offer your firm." He deferentially offered a clasp envelope.

Five days, he thought grimly, *to find a counterfeiter with more talent than a dyslexic apprentice draftsman, and this very impressive damned résumé undervalues me by half.* He didn't understand how it was to work; wouldn't Bourtzos simply contact the listed references, find them to be nonexistent, and see Steldan's imposture for what it was? But the contact man for the forger assured him that he would be believed. Steldan shrugged. Too much work had been put into it for it to be so simple a trap.

The deal he'd struck with the counterfeiter, in lieu of the cash he didn't have, was a willing acceptance of blackmail terms. The forger, with some intricate underworld connections, saw the value of having an inside man with the unswervingly honest Brantos, Brantos, and Bourtzos. Steldan felt that he had escaped from one trap only to fall into one that was deeper and more hopeless.

Bourtzos scanned the document carefully. Again he read it, more carefully, and once more. His smile faded. L. Tempes could not suppress a wince this time.

"This résumé is accurate?"

"It is."

"It does not account for your recent past."

"I have, indeed, fallen from my past prominence."

Bourtzos became harsh, in a low, direct voice. "Drugs? Crime? Were you in detention? Why should I waste my time?"

"I was hospitalized," Steldan lied.

"Indeed."

"I was inside the primary burst radius of the Block 10 explosion."

"Gods!" Bourtzos was startled despite himself. L. Tempes gasped audibly; to legitimize his eavesdropping, he was forced to enter the lobby and be introduced to "Mr. Tiernif."

"How did you survive?" asked Bourtzos, his curiosity overwhelming his hostility.

"A buttress interposed," Steldan answered with what he hoped was a convincing shudder. Until he'd met N. Wilth, the counterfeiter, he'd never heard of the Block 10 explosion. He still had no idea what exactly had exploded. Feigning reluctance, he continued. "My fiancée died in the explosion, and, losing hope, I let my affairs slide. I am ready now, however, to begin afresh. I wish to lend my services to your esteemed firm."

Bourtzos handed the résumé to Tempes, who reviewed it rapidly. "I can't give you an answer immediately," Bourtzos said, although his smile began to creep back onto his face. "I must confer with my partners, the

Mssrs. Brantos." His full reflex smile returned. "I think the answer may very well be 'yes.' "

Returning the résumé to Steldan, L. Tempes essayed a quiet: "Rather impressive, Mr. Tiernif. You would do well here."

"Return at two o'clock tomorrow, and we shall speak further." With a last glance at Steldan's damp, slightly crumpled outfit, he gestured the prospective employee to the door. Steldan left, congratulating himself on having found a comfortable occupation in which to hide.

To hide? Forever? That was not his intention. The part of his mind that constantly worked on long-range planning already fretted over his next moves. And yet for a time, all he could do was lie low.

He left the Spaceport office annex and passed into the bustling promenade. At the main reservations desk and at the boarding terminals, both below him on the main floor, he saw small clusters of security troopers, side-armed with tranquilizing pistols and sleep-gas grenades. The troopers appeared competent, yet bored: a standard peaceful Spaceport garrison. Steldan felt the tightness under his chest that a hunted man will feel, no matter how safe he may be for the moment. He wondered if he'd ever be free of it.

At the entrance to the central-city shuttle-tram, he met his contact from the counterfeiting ring.

"That didn't take long," Wilth observed. He was tall and slim, and reminded Steldan of a medical school cadaver. "Shall we hit it?"

"After you," Steldan agreed. Together they passed over the photoelectric turnstile and caught an unoccupied shuttle-tram. Wilth tapped onto a side panel the code for the City-South, where his employer—ultimately Steldan's employer as well—had his base.

"It would have been a lot easier," Steldan griped good-naturedly, "if you'd spotted me a better set of clothes."

"We wouldn't want to waste that kind of money until we trust you more," Wilth said, grinning. "Besides, I wanted to see how resourceful you could be."

They rode in silence for a time. Steldan watched the city pass by outside his window, and found himself impressed at the beauty of it. Technological abundance lived harmoniously with wide, naturalistic landscaping. Tall buildings stood peacefully among parks. The shuttle-tram took a gentle, winding course, passing often on narrow bridges over running water, clear and swift in imitation of mountain streams. Everywhere grew lush and varied greenery, grass-floored and tree-canopied.

Subtly, it was wrong. Steldan felt the stirrings of an unpleasant suspicion. This world wasn't yet old enough for this; the human colonization was only a few centuries along. Steldan's knowledge of colonial development argued against such advanced renewal.

"What was the Block 10 explosion?"

"It worked, didn't it?" Wilth smiled. Steldan was growing to dislike that smile.

"Mr. Bourtzos was impressed; awed even."

"The interplanetary freighter-tanker *Block 10*, loaded with 100,000 tons of reaction fuel from the midsystem refinery at Bleodh, lost its computer while landing. The pilot panicked. The ship landed—if 'landed' is the right word—going sixty-eight meters per second. They say you could hear it 4,000 kilometers away." He shook his head. "That was eleven months ago. Flattened a good third of the city. After that, there was rebuilding and landscaping, and they built a big monument at ground zero."

Steldan looked out at the scenery with a new respect. As big an event as it had been for this planet, he, at Naval Intelligence Central, hadn't heard a word of it.

"It was during the disruption and chaos that the boss was able to set up his organization. Drugs, guns, computer files, and, lucky for you, the best forgery operation on Chirkun."

Steldan managed to conceal his disgust. Wilth, oblivious, went on. "We did a bang-up job of switching identities. All of us legally died in the blast, so we're non-persons: harder to catch. If anybody needs a cover, we give 'em a name from the—"

"You mean the name I'm using, 'Ramo Tiernif . . .' "

"That's right: fried alias. With no surviving body to identify, why not?"

Steldan was appalled, and evidently was unable to hide it. Wilth's grin was mocking. "Don't like it, eh?"

"But you want to be thought dead, while I need to be legally alive, with an operant I.D., a computer record—"

"Same thing. The files were so mixed up that day, they're still not completely accurate. Oh, they're in pretty good shape, and it gets harder all the time, but there's still some leeway."

"While everyone else was putting out fires and carrying the wounded . . ."

"Me and the boss were pillaging the government files building."

"Sometimes it takes a disaster to bring out the best in people," Steldan sighed. Wilth ignored the sarcasm and just grinned maddeningly.

Disembarking, they walked for a few blocks through dense traffic, having arrived in the older, seamier section of the city, the City-South, where the criminals had built their lair. Steldan found himself affronted by the lawlessness of the area; crime not only thrived here, it advertised itself. Several of the men they passed were readily recognizable as lookouts. Steldan watched surreptitiously, but could not discover Wilth's pass-signal. Most likely the lookouts knew him by sight.

The older buildings they walked among had never been touched by the explosion; they were early colonial block-structures true to the rule. Together the two entered a large featureless building through heavy sliding doors, ascended a richly carpeted staircase, and advanced past more lookouts, who were probably bodyguards as well. Steldan sensed about them the almost imperceptible air that armed and dangerous men have.

"Wilth, why are you bringing me here? Aren't we safer dealing as before, through you as messenger?"

"Orders, pal. Here we are." He knocked on a thick door, which promptly swung open. Wilth motioned Steldan to enter. No one was in sight within.

"Aren't you coming?" asked Steldan.

"You go ahead. I report downstairs." Wilth waved and departed, trotting carelessly down the staircase.

Steldan looked into the room and saw a spare, utilitarian office, with a bare metal desk, phone system, and computer console. Hesitating for a moment, he took a breath and entered.

A soft hum sounded, and his body up to the chest was encased in an anticoncussion field, whose density he automatically catalogued as above .95. With his arms at his sides, in mid-stride, he was a fly in amber, a fish in ice.

He was doubly startled for having suspected the possibility of a trap of this kind, and yet having dismissed it as unlikely.

To his right a loudspeaker clicked, and out of it came the amplified voice of his captor.

"Navy!" spat the man. "You stink of it! It crawls from you!"

Steldan said nothing; nothing would have served. Part of his mind was analyzing the voice, trying to visualize the man behind it. He thought of an enormously fat man, scowling, a man with a vicious expression. He blinked, ridiculing this as mere guesswork, but the image remained.

"Give me one good reason I shouldn't send you back to them in pieces," the voice snarled.

"Because that's just what they'd like most," Steldan answered. There was a silence, and he knew his face was being watched, his words weighed. The field held him captive, helpless. He wondered if the energy drain was being monitored, if a security engineer would take notice. An anticoncussion field of this density bore a heavy cost in wattage; four men with truncheons could have held him no less securely.

He continued: "Your man Wilth followed me; did I go anywhere other than Brantos, Brantos, and Bourtzos? Blast it, I'm on the run!"

"But you *were* with the Navy, yes?" The voice had grown smooth, beguiling, dangerous.

"Yes, but—"

"Maybe with Naval Intelligence, hm?"

"I—" There was no answer for that one; the charge was true.

"Sent here to feel out my system, maybe?"

"No, sir, I—"

"You haven't made any glaring errors, and your approach when searching for a forger was believably clumsy, but"—he paused for emphasis—"but . . . I don't trust you! I have not survived this long amidst mistrust and treachery by allowing myself to trust people!

"You know the location of this building," the man continued. Steldan imagined him waving a corpulent arm. "That is no problem to me. I'm going to abandon it; have been planning to for months. You know Wilth. That's too bad for him! He's expendable. But you know too much. If you want to leave here alive, you'll tell me why I should trust you. Understand?!"

Adding *excitable* to his mental description of the man, Steldan tried to explain.

"I was with the Navy. But damn it, they're after me! I'm on the run, and it's my head if they catch me. I came to you for I.D., to help me hide."

"What did you do?"

"I . . . disobeyed . . ."

"That's a lie," the voice interrupted sharply.

"I—"

"That's another."

Steldan glared. "I coordinated a price-fixing scheme for Naval construction contracts. The damned ship was in mid-jump when the engine baffles denatured. No one died, but three engineers got pretty badly cooked. I heard about it in time, and ran."

There was a long silence. Then:

"It can be verified, of course?" The voice was studiously neutral, but Steldan knew better. His story had been swallowed, if only provisionally. His training as an interrogator had taught him how best to lie, and to get away with it.

"Name the ship," the voice suddenly demanded.

"The Assault Cruiser *Praesidium*," Steldan answered without hesitation. The *Praesidium* was scheduled for the scrap yards; should this man be interested enough to search that far, he would indeed find Steldan's name involved in the contracts. The Navy would be reticent about details; he could foresee no difficulties. Although much the same thoughts would be occurring to his captor, it was probably from thoroughness rather than true suspicion.

Another thought came to the hidden interviewer instead, and his voice over the speaker was intense. "You know price-fixing?"

Steldan nodded mutely.

"And Wilth fixed you a job with . . . ?"

"Brantos, Brantos, and Bourtzos, shipping brokers. And he didn't help me much, either."

"Your collateral was . . . vulnerability to blackmail?" Steldan heard the happy amazement permeating the voice. "Mr. Wilth has a positive talent for underestimating possibilities, that's all I can say." There was the sound of a chair being pushed back, of a man rising and pacing. Steldan heard another sound: that of keys on a computer keyboard being tapped rapidly. The anticoncussion field collapsed, leaving him staggering slightly, but free.

"Brantos, Brantos, and Bourtzos," the man repeated, sounding almost jovial. "I don't think Wilth has the vaguest notion of how much economic leverage they have."

"Whatever you've got in mind—"

"Yes?" snapped the voice.

"I hope it's subtle," Steldan weakly finished.

"For a while, you'll do nothing, beyond proving yourself to your employers. Then . . . Yes, subtlety is important in this game, never fear. I won't tell you my plans just yet, although you'll come to understand soon."

Steldan wondered where he'd made his worst mistake: running away, trusting Wilth, or applying for a broker's job. Once more he considered backing out and running again.

The voice continued, satisfied and happy. "They'll want you bonded, you know, and that'll take more than one of our common counterfeit résumés. I'll take care of that . . . As before, Wilth will be our go-between."

There followed more discussion, during which few specifics were made clear by the now-genial man. After that, Steldan was escorted through a back door and directed to a comfortable hotel near the Spaceport.

Through the long night he listened to the intermittent thunder of Spaceships being boosted into orbit by the Port's gigantic landing grid. He imagined the ascent of the slim Couriers, the massive Liners, the arrowhead Scouts; he dreamed of everyone on the planet taking ship and leaving him on a windswept, grassy field, cold and alone.

Steldan passed most of the next morning at the Spaceport, studying the arrival and departure schedules, learning of the freighter firms and the rival brokerage houses, and familiarizing himself with the customs and import bureaucracy. He also learned enough about the Military Airspace and Close Orbit flight control systems to leave him substantially more worried than he had been. Had his pilot been intercepted on takeoff? Had he been captured, questioned? Did they know who they were looking for, and why? Port security seemed normal, with only the few bored guards standing sentry at sensitive locations.

Some quick calculations at a coin-operated computer in the Port promenade waiting room assured him that his trace radiation dosage had by now dissipated. Even when he'd received it—and he swore never again to trust a pilot in a hurry—he'd known it wouldn't be a health hazard.

At two o'clock he presented himself at the offices of Brantos, Brantos, and Bourtzos. With the cash lent him by Wilth he had attired himself more appropriately, and his appearance elicited an almost sincere smile from John Bourtzos.

Steldan was motioned to an overstuffed chair, and waited patiently while Bourtzos summoned his partners from a rear office. They soon returned, and he rose deferentially.

"Mr. Tiernif, this is Arve Brantos, and Arve Brantos Jr. Mssrs. Brantos, this is Ramo Tiernif, applying for a position as a Junior Clerk."

The elder Brantos, a stiffly formal man of about eighty, speared Steldan with strangely intense eyes. After a moment the tall, cragged, and gnarled patriarch nodded sharply, once. Without further concern he straightened, thrust his hands deep within the pockets of his tailored brown suit, and strode from the room.

The younger Brantos was a man of appearance so commonplace that even the well-trained Steldan had difficulty fixing his features. About fifty, he wore his gold-brown suit with ease, clasping his hands together before him. He looked over the prospective clerk with a neutral glance, and nodded also, more slowly and meaningfully. He looked over to Bourtzos and smiled a crisp little smile of approval.

Bit by bit, Steldan recalled the workings of the shadow-show of etiquette, which was how things were done in the private sector. After the rigors of military protocol, he found the amenities here abstract and unpleasantly vague.

"I have examined your résumé," Brantos said, his voice evenly modulated, "and find it attractive. I find no reason for doubt. Present yourself at four today at First-list Bondsmen with adequate documentation. You will be working here with Senior Clerk Tempes."

Tempes entered the room at that point, as if coincidentally leaving the files cubicle. Steldan smiled inwardly, appreciating a man with such stage presence combined with an almost perfectly straight face. On the other hand, this would be a man to beware of, if illegal procedures were to be a part of his occupation.

"I will be glad to have you working under my supervision," he said, and smiled a very sincere smile at Steldan. His eyes, however, were sharp and alert, the eyes of a man who is, first and foremost, observant.

For the third time, Steldan considered leaving the plush offices, fleeing the mixed city, perhaps escaping altogether from the world of Chirkun. He felt the urge to start again, to run away from this increasingly complicated refuge. The job promised comfort, however, in return for the type of risks he'd not be able to avoid in any case.

Inside a week he was familiar with the firm's filing and bookkeeping systems, and was regaining competence with the computerized data retrieval file. L. Tempes felt that the new clerk would go far.

Inside a month, Wilth gave him his first list of coded, illegal instructions.

Lieutenant Ron Gray of Concordat Naval Intelligence sat in the antechamber of the office of the Vice-President (Security) of the planet Chirkun. Mastering his impatience and nervousness, he managed to sit motionless, as if he were keeping the Vice-President waiting, rather than being kept on ice himself. He sat ramrod straight, crisp in his black-and-gray uniform, occasionally reaching up casually to brush his regulation—and not a millimeter more—moustache of light brown. His clear blue eyes swept the room repeatedly.

The door opened from within and a bodyguard-secretary leaned out, beckoning the Lieutenant. "Vice-President Nielsen will see you now."

Entering brusquely, Lieutenant Gray gave the bodyguard a curt dismissing gesture, and was mildly surprised to find it obeyed. He stopped and looked about. The office was huge, decorated in blues and greens. Indirectly lighted, with a dimly glowing aquarium set into one wall, the office reminded him of an undersea grotto, perhaps with something large and slimy lurking at the back. He felt certain that the dim light hid his furtive shudder.

"Lieutenant Gray." It was a greeting.

"Sir," Gray blurted, twitching in his effort not to salute.

"I understand you're after a fugitive."

Gray nodded.

"How can we help you?"

Asked a question within his field, Gray regained some of his natural competence. "I'll want some help with a computer search, and a general all-points bulletin with your local enforcement agencies. I'd like a liaison officer from your Central Intelligence Bureau, who will report to me at my temporary office at the Spaceport." He reached into his folder and pulled out a sheaf of papers; he handed them clumsily to the Vice-President. "Here is the Concordat warrant, the Naval warrant, the fugitive's file, and his photo."

The Vice-President scanned each carelessly. Lieutenant Gray continued, somewhat unevenly: "I won't need much more than a low-level alert; he's not dangerous. I'll organize the Spaceport security systems so that he can't escape off-planet."

Nielsen shifted himself in his chair and peered more carefully at the photograph. " 'Athalos Steldan.' What did he do?"

"That's not important," Gray quickly said. Even he hadn't been told that part. "Are the warrants in order?"

"Yes. How do you know he's here?"

"We have the ship that brought him here, although its pilot got away. The Auto-log was sealed, and when opened showed a three-minute setdown here."

"That doesn't make any sense," objected the trim Vice-President. "Why couldn't your Steldan have been the pilot himself?"

"Athalos Steldan could no more have piloted a spaceship than he could have flown here with wax wings. And piloting's not a skill you can pick up on the sly."

Hesitantly, the Vice-President admitted, "We did track a ship setting down, for about three minutes. We thought it was just another smuggling run."

"That's exactly what it was. Smuggling in a person." Gray kept his thoughts hidden, but it struck him with some shock. *They have a smuggling problem that they can do nothing about? Perhaps this world could use some cleaning up.*

"I'll see that you get what you've asked for . . . I'll attach a computer worker to you, and perhaps a liaison from the C.I.B. We are somewhat understaffed . . ."

You must be, Gray thought. "Excellent." He saluted, cursed himself silently for doing so, turned, and left the office.

Crossing the town on the shuttle-tram, his thoughts were upon Steldan. The fugitive's crime was yet a mystery, but from the psychological profile he'd been given, he felt that he almost knew him as a person. Athalos Steldan. For some reason, the word that described him best was "precise." No pedantic perfectionist, yet never lax, he was an intrinsically lazy man, of the type who gets the most work done when that work simplifies tasks for him in the future. Gray, eager and compulsive, found it difficult to appreciate truly industrious laziness.

Steldan. A man of cities, someone who is unhappy when there's no filing system at hand, no reference library within reach. One born to books, and whose physique, barely on the healthy side of average, is due more to his heredity than to exercise.

According to these reports, Steldan was popular among both his superiors and his underlings, despite a quixotic tendency toward overly individualistic action. In that, he seemed to be out of place in the regimentation of the Navy, and his promotion hearings were eventful testimonies to his precipitancy.

The tram discharged Gray on the second level of the Spaceport promenade; he looked long at the bustling lower level. Pedestrians milled; Marines on leave trooped in supporting pairs, slaves to habit. Small shops and restaurants, beneath lit signs of twinkling lights, breathed customers in, let them out. Planters held small gardens, loop-fronded indoor trees, spiky desert rock-clinging vines that emitted a vague perfume.

Would Steldan be attracted to this colorful and dense dance of people? No. Gray realized, with a self-conscious trace of humor, that Steldan would prefer the view from right here, above the crowd, watching what he would always be too self-conscious to join.

Gray moved along at last, rounding the end of the promenade balcony and entering the close-corridored maze of the office annex. At the disburser's station he obtained a key, and from there he had little difficulty in finding his door. The office that he'd been assigned was acceptable, if small. Bare walls, thin carpeting, and recessed lighting gave it a grim appearance; the two desks, separated by a flimsy room divider, bore computer-links, with no terminals. An empty file-station reminded him of the labor awaiting him.

The office was almost exactly one flight below those of Brantos, Brantos, and Bourtzos. Soon Lieutenant Gray, with his C.I.B. computer expert and liaison, had organized a tight, globe-spanning search-net, casting actively for the fugitive who was hiding less than ten meters away.

* * *

"Wilth, you dog, you're asking too much." Steldan fought to keep his voice low as he spoke with his contact in the city's second-finest restaurant. Wilth, he knew, felt as out of place here as Steldan had felt in the back alleys of the old City-South.

"The plan is simple. What do you want?" Wilth's hand hovered over the implements of the table setting, and selected one indecisively. "Price-fixing is straightforward, and you're in the best place to do it."

" 'Subtle,' your boss said." Steldan gestured curtly to forestall Wilth's protest. "This scheme is as subtle as a highjacking. If you give me two days, I can do the same thing in a far less brutal fashion."

"What's so brutal? You just enter a low bid, then vacate it at the unsealing. Right?"

"Straight out of the textbook," Steldan said, unsmiling. "Would you care to put it into practice?"

Wilth tasted his meal experimentally, and found it to his liking. Around a mouthful, he argued, "The boss maybe wants it this way. He gave me the chart; you obey. Or else he goes to the city police. See?"

"No." Steldan, with the correct fork, cut into his own meal, offering Wilth a subtle lesson in etiquette. Wilth didn't notice. "If he wants to drive down the price of these imports, I can do it for him. It will simply take time."

"Boss said do it today; you got five hours left."

Steldan resolved to slip out and leave Wilth with the check. The skinny counterfeiter could pay for it . . . and would almost certainly make a spectacle of himself doing so. It would be a mild enough revenge. "If that's the way it has to be, then I'll do it. By tomorrow, you'll have a fixed price contract on the radios, mild steel, and blank data tapes."

"And the surgical lasers," Wilth insisted. "Don't you dare forget those."

Steldan sighed heavily. "I'll go take care of it, then," he snapped, and quietly rose, heading for the exit.

"Hey!" Wilth howled, and all eyes in the crowded dining room turned on him with annoyance. Abashed, fuming, he returned to his meal.

Steldan's satisfaction was short-lived; by the time

he'd reached the street his concern had surfaced again. Stepping across the slideway, he reached the shuttle-tram and keyed for the Spaceport. *A purchase order,* he mused, *and a transshipments request. . .* Fairly easy to do, but requiring a few minutes' access to the computer-files and to Bourtzos' verification coder. The offices of Brantos, Brantos, and Bourtzos were not laid out with privacy in mind.

He disembarked at the Spaceport Promenade, and found himself again impressed with the five-tiered arcade's appearance of orderly chaos. From the shuttle-tram station, past the embarkation gates, and on to the many small shops sprinkling the large hall, thousands of people hurried, tarried, moved in shifting patterns up and down the Spaceport's heart.

Riding an ascensor to the third tier, Steldan walked briskly toward the Annex, and his employers and victims.

"You're back early," greeted Tempes. "Was the restaurant to your liking?"

"Completely; I've seldom enjoyed a meal as much." He'd grown to like Tempes, and to profit from his advice. On the other hand, he'd been unable to ferret out any trace of whimsy in the studious senior clerk, no sense of humor at all.

"How did it compare with similar meals—'Centerspace,' as you Navy chaps say?"

Instantly Steldan was on alert; his forged papers had nowhere indicated his connections with the Concordat Navy. As casually as possible—even to him it sounded forced—he answered: "Favorably. The spices were subtle, yet present . . . How did you guess that I'd been in the Navy?"

"It was just that: a guess. You tend to use words like 'Centerspace,' 'uplink,' and so forth, and the honorific 'sir' comes easily to you."

"Aye. I took Naval Officer's Training Cadre at University, and served a year"—he grinned—"in an enlistment depot." *I'm overcloaked in lies,* he groaned to himself, and almost missed Tempes' next question.

"What, then, is your homeworld?"

"My homeworld?" *Wasn't that on the résumé?* "Thierry-Danege. A small world, so far from here you can't see its sun."

"So far? Dozens of parsecs?" Tempes smiled, and looked at Steldan as if seeing him for the first time. "I'm glad you're here."

"And I. And now, back to work."

"Since you're here to watch things, I'll step out for my own lunch. Mr. Bourtzos will be back at one."

"Everything will be fine," Steldan agreed, both relieved and worried by his good fortune. Tempes nodded, and exited briskly.

Steldan did not immediately loot Bourtzos' cubicle, but first set up the coded arrangements on the computer file. With his heart pounding, he rose, crossed to his employer's desk, and quietly lifted the coder. Back at his own cubicle he pressed the coder into the matching slot on the file, and tapped the SEND key.

Only then did he realize what Wilth's master—his own master—could want with surgical lasers.

Returning the coder to Bourtzos' desk, his eyes and ears were back at the bright room at the Naval Intelligence School. The instructor, tall, crane-like, bald as an egg and as pale, had just remarked that a surgical laser was the second-best instrument of torture known.

"What, then, is the best?" he had asked, and Steldan had quietly answered: "A two-inch straightpin."

"Torture," he now mumbled, and shivered. His blackmailers had his correct name. They had his record. They knew that he had medical training, that he was, in fact, a doctor. They would want him to be their expert torturer.

Anxiously he searched for alternatives. Could the lasers be for lockpicking? Cutting lasers were far cheaper. Microwelding? Microwelders. Surgery? Not in secret. But torture . . . torture . . .

He almost phoned Wilth. Gingerly he broke the connection before it was completed. By no means would Wilth tell him, even if he really knew. Persuading himself that it was a misunderstanding, afraid that it wasn't, he returned to his work.

Ron Gray sipped quietly at his mug of hot chocolate, and studied the map of the city. *Either the South Slums or the Spaceport,* he repeated to himself, nodding absently. *He's using the identity and papers of a victim of the Block 10 explosion. I know where he's not, and I have a good idea of where he is.* Unfortunately, his investigations hadn't proceeded very far beyond these obvious facts in the several weeks he'd been here.

Harcourt, his C.I.B. liaison and computer technician, had moved mountains, if only of red tape, and had coordinated the planetwide search diligently. Gray, with Concordat clearance, had worked his own miracles, blocking avenues of escape; leaving others carefully open, and carefully trapped; monitoring airspace and close orbit space. That Steldan couldn't leave the way he'd come, by a secretively landing and boosting spacecraft, was guaranteed by the constant vigilance of two Serpent-Class Scouts on 24-hour patrol. Tied by high-level codeword into the security systems aboard all off-planet traffic, these ships sealed the planet absolutely. They also had Gray badly worried.

Why do they want him? What did he do?

His original order: "Capture and conduct to Sector Headquarters Captain Athalos Steldan," had been changed, first to: "Capture if possible and by all means prevent escape of Captain Athalos Steldan," then to the personal instructions from Commodore Higgins, Chief of Investigations: "Capture him or kill him; do not let him escape. Do not listen to anything he may say."

Appended to that dispatch was a note from Commander Finch, Gray's immediate superior: "Hell popping up here. Find A.S. or heads will roll."

Soon thereafter the two Scoutships had shown up, with orders to assist Gray in any way. What concerned him the most, however, (next to the suggestive "Do not listen to anything he may say") was the report he'd received yesterday stating that Commodore Rudolfs, Steldan's immediate superior, was in detention, his affairs being handled by Admiral Horst's staff.

Gray dug into his memory: Admiral Horst, Chief of Naval Intelligence, appointed by the Secretary of the Navy, Grand Admiral Telford himself. *Ah, Captain Steldan, what have you gotten yourself into?*

Pushing the map and his speculations aside, he finished his chocolate and tried to order his thoughts. *Get inside the quarry's head; imagine what you'd do if you were running. Think the way he must now be thinking.* But that, he knew, was impossible; to successfully think like a running man, one must *be* a running man. Nevertheless . . .

South Slums: noisy, unstructured, complex. Spaceport: noisy, structured, complex. Both were cities within the city; both offered hiding places, information nets, retreat routes . . .

Pride made the decision for Gray. *If he's here, under my nose, and I don't get him, then I'm going to look like a prize fool.*

"Harcourt!" he called. The C.I.B. liaison, a slightly overweight woman, thirtyish, blonde and red-cheeked, answered abstractedly, poking her head over the partition that split the office.

"Yeah?"

"Um . . . We're going to concentrate on the Spaceport for a while. He might be closer than I've thought."

"Right. Let me kill this run . . . okay, go ahead."

"Image recognition scanners at all entrances and exits."

"Right. Optic or Sonic?"

"Deep sonic; he might have grown a beard or something, but his facial bone structure . . ."

"He *was* a surgeon . . ."

"How would he do facial surgery on himself?" Gray snorted.

"Or maybe he's lost a couple of fistfights."

Ignoring that, Gray continued: "Automatic scanning of all I.D. cards—"

"We already have that, at all exits, entrances, and at the boarding gates."

"Well, code the system to watch for any card with no activity on it between the Block 10 explosion and thirteen weeks ago."

"Bet we catch a few tax evaders, too. I wonder if that's admissable evidence . . ."

"Have an isotope spray mounted over each possible exit, so we can tag him if he runs. Double the guards —no! Strike that. He's too likely to notice."

"Plainclothesmen."

"Maybe . . . but we'd need quite a few, with long cycles. He's clever, this Steldan."

After settling another dozen minor points, Gray returned to his papers while Harcourt departed for the Portmaster's offices to relay the arrangements. The imperfectly damped rumble of a departing liner filled the wide corridors, halting speech and rolling an occasional pencil off a desk or tabletop. Only a few people stood near the Portmaster's, and Harcourt was detained only briefly before being passed behind the counter to the inner chambers.

She passed within three meters of Athalos Steldan, who was conversing quietly with an orbit-control clerk at the counter.

"I lost two cousins to the *Block 10*—who didn't?" The pink-faced clerk, a glint in his eye belying the somber tale, was cheerful, open, almost boastful, and very talkative. "Sure, I was mad—weren't we all? But we need the fuel, and tankers are the only way to get it here.

"Y'see, the way orbits work, you can't be completely safe. There's no way to land something that big smoothly. But we've added a lot of safeguards, different orbit approaches, and lots of destruct triggers, so we can explode 'em in midair, if they start to fall."

"Why not land them in the desert, or at sea?" asked Steldan, knowing full well the answer. With only the slightest of nudges, the conversation had moved directly, if slowly, to the point that he needed.

"You've been out on the observation deck? You saw those big concentric hexagons marked on the concrete? That's a three-hundred hectare boost and landing grid. For both taking off and grounding, that thing saves one-and-a-half tons of fuel for every ton of spaceship."

"The ships don't do the work—"

"—*It* does. Right. And sure, fuel's free, out there. But shipping it . . . wow!"

"So you're saving, um, sixty percent on fuel?"

"Sixty-seven percent plus, when you count the weight of the ship. And those things are *built*. Armored, partitioned, vented, baffled—the drive out on a pole— Tell me.

How much do you think that'd help, building them like battleships?" The clerk grinned at Steldan challengingly.

"Well—"

"It wouldn't help at all! She crashes, she explodes. Thirty megacredits worth of 'safety features' and they're not worth heck. But the public demanded it. 'Make 'em safe,' they yowled, and so they armor-plated 'em. Only two things make sense: the destruct trigger—which won't work in the last six minutes, 'cause airbursts are worse than ground explosions—and the orbit changes."

About which we'll speak further, Steldan thought. "Do you think the public still fears another explosion?"

The clerk gave an exaggerated grimace. "You're not even allowed to *joke* about it. Everybody does, but there's a five hundred credit fine for telling Block 10 jokes in public. And for real false alarms, you can be locked up for thirty days to four years."

"I'll be careful."

"You'd better be. In fact—"

"Excuse me; you've got a light flashing on your console."

The clerk looked away, turned back. "That's just the automatic navigation check on the liner that boosted a few minutes ago. Here." He tapped an instruction onto his console, and pushed the machine around on its base so Steldan could see more easily. "That's a graphic of the ship's orbit . . . That's the elapsed time, three minutes, seven seconds; eight; nine—That's the six orbital elements, changing 'cause she's on positive drive . . . This here shows that the computer's watching and all's well."

"Does this machine do simulations?"

"Yeah. Like to see one?"

"Um . . . can you show me the new fuel tanker approach?"

"Easy. Here," he said as he typed in a short sequence.

That, Steldan decided twenty minutes later, *was the easiest interrogation of my career.*

At the offices of Brantos, Brantos, and Bourtzos, he found the ever-crisp Tempes bogged down in a priority dispute with the owners of two competing import firms. The older, a soft man in a polished white suit, was glaring at a younger man, evidently the owner and pilot of a one-ship speculating concern. Tempes, by remaining entirely calm himself, was slowly placating the gentlemen, only to see them turn and shout again, trying to sway Steldan to their cause.

"Mr. Bourtzos—I assume you are Mr. Bourtzos—you must listen to me! I'm being robbed—" whined the older man in a thin voice. His moist eyes begged for sympathy.

"I flew the whole way from Ballerthy with this shipment," drawled the pilot, throwing his chest out and tensing his arms, "and I don't expect to dump it—"

Steldan executed a quick half-bow to the first man and caught the hand of the pilot in a hearty handshake. In an almost dance-like maneuver, Tempes stepped between the two competitors and gestured to his right, discreetly herding the first complainant to a chair, while Steldan pushed—without pushing at all—the pilot toward his cubicle.

"Be seated," Steldan offered, and lowered himself to his chair. The empty desk top stood between the pilot and himself, giving them emotional as well as physical separation. The pilot looked about, then fixed his sharp gaze on Steldan.

"From Ballerthy to here," the pilot continued, "two hundred hours listenin' to my engines purr, carryin' my dang shipment, and *he*"—a gesture toward Tempes— "tells me he's buyin' 'em from oily-face in the white suit."

"Something—"

"I don't mind the hazards of Jumpspace. I don't even mind the two Patrol ships upstairs . . ." Steldan's face must have changed expression. "Yeah, a Patrol. As if this backwater nowhere world needed looking over. They let me through with no trouble, but from the look of things, I'm in for a real searchin' when I leave."

"Planetary Cutters?" Steldan asked quietly.

"Hell no; Serpents! Concordat Scouts, and armed like it was war."

"Indeed." Steldan's throat seemed slightly dry.

The pilot leaned back and kicked his well-polished boots up on top of the desk. "And me with a cargo hold full of rare fissionables." He gave Steldan a meaningful look.

Steldan could only breathe a sigh of relief; he'd been deathly afraid the man would say "surgical lasers."

"Have you got your papers handy?" he asked routinely. *Two Scouts on blockade,* he mused. *But it's too late. What's done is done, and I can't undo it. Would I if I could?* he wondered.

After some private consultation with Tempes, Steldan was able to make a marginally satisfactory offer to the pilot, who stalked off snarling, accepting the deal with poor grace, and wondering how he'd pay for ship's fuel.

The late afternoon turned slowly to dusk, the silence of the Spaceport Annex split twice by departing spacecraft. In her half of the small office, Harcourt worked with nearly hypnotic concentration at the computer-search for the fugitive Steldan. She didn't notice when Gray bid her good evening; she completely lost track of the hour.

The problem—cross-indexing the searches to eliminate every entry save one—was endlessly fascinating to her. The pure logic was intellectually consuming.

Entry after entry flashed onto her blue screen, moving, it sometimes seemed, with lives of their own. Names, serial numbers, phone codes, and more names.

And each of those names belongs to a person who died in that damned explosion.

The thought sobered her. Endless thousands of names, victims all, who had the misfortune, that one day, to be too close to the place the *Block 10* chanced to hit.

What made them different from anyone else? she wondered. *What lets some survive, while others die?*

Steldan, she decided, was a survivor. Perhaps it was a mild hallucination, born of the late hour and her long effort, but she almost felt she knew him. How many times had she held him in her hand, here in this list of names, only to lose him? Her fingers were simply too short and fat to make proper god-like claws, reaching spectrally out over the city . . .

She felt differently about this Steldan than about anyone else she'd ever tried to track down, if for no other reason than that thus far he'd eluded her. No one else, she thought smugly, had ever lasted longer than two weeks, once she was on the job.

He's intelligent. He's educated. He's not headstrong, but he's unremittingly individual. Some people are too stupid to know when to quit; I've got more respect for this fellow than to believe it of him.

Where has he gotten to?

She looked at his photo, and tried to read his mind from it. He wore his black-and-gray uniform comfortably, but her eye saw him, and not it. The collar was tight beneath his chin, his hair was neatly combed into place; Harcourt saw his individuality, his uniqueness, despite these clues.

He had a wide face with a slightly upturned nose, compressed lips, a dreamer's brow . . .

Where was he? What was he thinking?

Harcourt shook her head. This had suddenly become a personal challenge, and there was nothing she delighted in more than that. To the gods with logic! She sat before her computers, shoulders straight, jaw firmly set, and played every hunch she could think of.

Again and again she cast her net out over the database, the long graveyard list of the dead victims of the city-scorching explosion. Again and again she diced with the overwhelming odds against her.

And on her thirty-third try, she caught him.

"Lieutenant Gray?" she called aloud. There was no answer.

"Oh, drat, what time is it?" She fumbled for the phone, her eyes painfully readjusting to the room light. Gray answered her call on the second ring.

"Yes?"

"Harcourt here. I think I've got him."

"What? How?"

"Unless you know of a way for a man to be in two places at once, a guy named 'Ramo Tiernif' took the Block 10 explosion at two distances, and either died, or did not die."

"Or both," Gray muttered.

"He was recently bonded by First-List Bondsmen for a job with an import broker. I've got the file."

"I'll be there as soon as I can," Gray snapped. "Contact the broker—at his home! We'll hit the office at once."

"Sure thing." She rang off. Lieutenant Gray might

be a bit standoffish and maladroit, but he could be a man of action when it was necessary.

Looking a last time at Steldan's photograph, she felt a pang of regret. It had been a glorious chase, and she was almost sorry to have it finished.

At six, Tempes rose from his keyboard and eased into his coat. Steldan remained seated at his own console. Tempes raised an eyebrow in inquiry. Steldan gestured helplessly at his unfinished paperwork. Smiling, bowing formally, Tempes turned, strode grandly out the door, and turned to lock it and smile through the thick, blue-tinted glass. Steldan waved, knowing that he was never again to see the affable senior clerk.

On his console he wiped off the work in progress and prefixed a new order:

REFINERY BETA-INSYSTEM/
DELIVERY FORTY THOUSAND TONS REFINED FUEL/
ONE TANKER AS AVAILABLE METROYAN'S SYSTEM FREIGHT/
SHIP IMMEDIATELY UPON RECEIPT OF CODEWORD "INTERROGATE"/
TO SPACEPORT LEONIDAS CITY: GROUND AT LOCAL NOON///

He then retrieved the verification coder, coded the order, sent it, and prefixed and coded an instruction to forget the previous order. It wouldn't fool a computer expert, but it gave him the time he needed.

I've gotten in too deep. Organized crime, alibis for my alibis, and deceiving my basically honest employers. I'll risk the thirty-day to four-year jail sentence.

His plan was fairly simple. In a few days he'd send the codeword to the refinery Beta-insystem, and at the next Spaceport noon the bulk transport would approach the planet in an elaborately contrived spiral. Checks and counter-checks would ensure that the landing was safe, and yet, despite all the security, the Spaceport would be jammed with frightened people demanding that the landing be aborted. Steldan would be able to assure this: He had the phone listings of the seventeen citizen's committees, clubs, and parties that currently protested any landing of fuel on Chirkun at all. Messages to them, suitably phrased, would guarantee a good turnout. In the confusion, while protesters and security forces clustered at the landing field and at the Portmaster's offices, Steldan would have little trouble escaping through the crush. It seemed the best diversion to get him clear of Wilth, Bourtzos, and the Navy.

He'd had enough of this city and its intrigues. It was to the spacelanes with him, to hide in the smallest, out-of-the-way world he could find, and in the role of an unskilled laborer. Ramo Tiernif would die again.

For now . . . Grasping the phone, he punched out Wilth's code. Rather to his surprise, Wilth answered.

"Yes?" His voice was parched, mechanical, partly from drugs, Steldan decided, and partly from anti-linetap devices attached to his phone, distorting the signal.

"Ramo Tiernif here; are you busy?"

"Where are you calling from?"

"The offices of Brantos, Brantos, and Bourtzos."

"Umm . . . O.K., we can talk safely, I guess. What's digging at you?"

"The surgical lasers—"

"Have you always been this stupid, or were you trained to it?" Wilth snarled.

"This line," Steldan explained icily, "is safe. I'm not tapped. You're not tapped. So . . ."

"All right; all right. So?"

"I know what you intend to use them for."

"Big stinking deal. We've done it before, and we'll do it again. We used to use scalpels. It's nothing special, if you can get the talent. You, by the way, have the talent. It's on your Navy records."

"You torture people all the time," Steldan stated, somewhat numbly.

"Torture? No, dummy, surgery! To change people's faces!" He paused for a few seconds. "Although they'd make *dandy* torture instruments . . ."

"Wilth, you ogre—"

"Yeah," Wilth gleefully agreed. "Listen up. I might as well tell you now, seeing as how you're on such a secure line and all. You're the talent. Boss figures not to let you go to waste. We want new faces. You're the surgeon. You operate, while some guys stand watch, in case something should accidentally happen . . . Do you understand?"

"I can't do that. There are a thousand reasons that I can't do it. Sepsis, support, anesthesia . . . Do you have any idea how delicate facial surgery *is?*"

"No," Wilth drawled, making it clear that he didn't care. No one, after all, was going to mess with *his* face; he wasn't part of the idiotic plan.

"It cannot be done."

"You'll have some time to figure it out. You'll think of something."

Interrupting Steldan's hostile reply came a savage reverberation: the pounding of heavy boots on the blue glass doors of the brokerage offices. Slamming down the phone, he leaped up to see a knot of armed men outside in the hallway: Spaceport security men, led by Lieutenant Ron Gray. The door was again kicked, and again vibrated, but did not open or shatter.

Diving for a desk drawer, Steldan reached inside as if drawing a weapon, then turned and dashed toward the rear offices. Pulling back to shelter, the troopers momentarily halted their assault on the door, then returned, two heavy soldiers lifting their boots for a solid kick.

Stun guns, glue grenades, tranquilizer and sleep-gas weapons, Steldan thought swiftly: *crowd-control and peacetime arms.* The doors shivered, held, shivered, held. *Air ducts? Too small. Windows? None.* He darted into the conference room, locked the door, and whirled about, looking for an avenue of escape. Outside, he heard the glass doors shatter to a final kick. Ducking, weaving, the soldiers entered, spread, searched in supporting pairs.

At once all sounds ceased, and an angry voice penetrated the stillness. "Who is responsible for this outrage?"

Steldan recognized Arve Brantos Jr., and decided that the interruption was good for a very few moments. He looked about once more. The dimly lit room was dominated by the featureless conference table, circular, three meters across. Seven luxurious chairs upholstered in soft gray fabric surrounded it, and above it hung a chandelier, now unlit, of crystal and fine-grained wood. Surrounding the square room, hiding the walls, were curtain-panels of a pale-green fabric. A detail of the chandelier's ceiling mount riveted Steldan, and with a pang he realized that the ceiling was of easily crumbled fiberboard panels.

Working swiftly, he removed one of the curtains, and with the curtain rod he punctured a man-sized hole in the ceiling above the table. As he had suspected, he found a meter-wide space between the ceiling and the solid surface of the next level's floor. Could a person move up there, and escape? The space was full of piping and wiring conduits, and the brittle panels underfoot were untrustworthy, but there seemed to be room . . .

He leaped from the table and caught a 3-cm pipe. Pulling himself up into the unlit cavity he saw how the chandelier was securely anchored to the second ceiling, and that the mount visible from below was purely decorative.

The pipe he crawled onto next, a meter away, was a counter-current cooling pipe, and even through his clothing he felt its heat. Quickly moving crabwise, trying for silence, he followed it into the darkness. Soon he hit an obstruction, and realized that the walls of the office suites must reach completely to the true ceiling, although the individual cubicle and office walls stopped at the lower surface. By dead reckoning he decided he was above the shattered glass of the front office doors; he could go no further up here.

From below he heard Brantos calling: "Tiernif! *Tiernif!*"

A different voice superseded him: that of the intelligence officer that had tracked the quarry here. "Steldan! Come out! We have a warrant for you! You won't be harmed! Surrender!"

Sweat flashed to Steldan's forehead. "Never!" he shouted, and with a shower of crumbling ceiling panels he crashed through to the glass-strewn carpet, knocking a security man to his knees, and himself rolling on shoulder and hip through the door. For a second he lay numb, the soldiers stood shocked; then Steldan was on his feet, moving down the hallways at top speed.

Past bewildered citizens he flashed, followed by a fleet pack of well-armed soldiery. Ahead he saw a bank of elevators, and that the doors of one were closing. A dash, a leap, and he flew headlong through the doors, which closed on his ankles. Sensing the obstruction, they hastily opened again. With a groan, Steldan stabbed the *Close Doors* button set conveniently low on the control panel, and yanked his feet inside. The elevator began to ascend.

At the fourth floor, the car stopped, and the doors slid halfway open. A red light blinked on over the control panel, and the doors began to shut. By that time Steldan was out of the car, ankles and all. His pursuers had been damned quick with an override key.

He found himself in unfamiliar territory, among the lower rent offices. Ahead, two corridors intersected, offering him some choice. There were no witnesses. The Spaceport was much like a small city, nested within the larger confines of Leonidas city. Hiding places could be found, with a little ingenuity, that might require weeks of intensive search to be revealed. The Concordat had those weeks—although possibly not much more—and if Commodore Higgins or Admiral Horst ever caught him, death by ionization would be more kind.

For now: run. He turned left and ran down the empty corridor soon approaching another intersection, Y-shaped. *How do I leave the Spaceport completely?* Left again. *They'll be at the elevator station by now, spreading out.* Ahead, moving night air suggested an open window; rounding a bend, he found a balcony opening to his left. Ducking onto it, he oriented himself. He was on the side of the Spaceport Annex away from the main boost-grid, and overlooking the construction yards and fuel storage tanks. Far away, behind the bright lights and towering gantries, he could see the warm glow of the City-South. He looked over the railing: twelve meters straight down to a poorly lit patio. On each floor beneath him, an identical balcony protruded.

Why not? he wondered, and swung himself over the railing. Carefully he lowered himself until he hung onto the balcony's deck with his fingers. Swing out, swing in, and let go . . . He landed roughly on the floor of the third level balcony, safely inside the railing. It was a simple trick, requiring only that one had no particular fear of heights. Once again, he clambered over the rail, lowered himself, swung, dropped. His landing was unbalanced, and he sprawled into a deck chair.

"Who's there?" called a voice from inside the building. Steldan hastily climbed over the rail and dropped the last level. From above, the voice muttered something perplexed. Plainly the man had not been a security trooper. Crossing the patio, Steldan pushed through a high hedge, dark green and mildly prickly. Kicking himself free of it, he jumped down a half-meter embankment to a deserted access and service road, brightly lit by a blazing yellow streetlamp. The road, for as far as he could see in either direction, ran between the tall greenery and a high concrete wall. Dashing across the way, he leaped, caught the top of the wall, and scrambled atop it. On the other side was a maze of storage buildings, black-roofed, each of them locked. The ground level here was another two meters below that of the roadway.

He leaped onto the nearest roof, and slipped, losing his footing on the waterproofed surface, landing heavily on his back. He lay still for a while, breathing deeply. The cool air bathed his face; the calm silence of the deserted warehouse-yard lulled him. It was hard for him truly to appreciate that he had been chased, harder to realize that he'd eluded his pursuers. *Maybe I'll just lie here, and sleep, and in the morning* . . . He drew a deep breath and rolled onto his knees. Shaking his head, he crawled to the edge of the roof and peered down into darkness. The gap was too wide to leap; he rolled over into the cleft. Again he hung by his fingers; again he dropped, landing heavily on bruised feet, sore legs. *My clothing has had it,* he judged, feeling cool air on his knees.

Making his way past the looming warehouses, he proceeded toward the construction yards. Soon he came to a clear view. *My luck holds average,* he decided; there was perhaps half a kilometer of clear concrete between him and the construction outbuildings, and yet there were no floodlamps, and, most important, no dividing fence. He forced himself into a brisk jog across the flat expanse.

Skirting the construction area proper, he came at last to the Spaceport security fence away from the fuel tanks. Thirty meters high, of woven one-piece wire-net, and rotten with alarm sensors, the fence was impassable. Steldan sat on a discarded section of half-meter pipe and shuddered, wishing he could just give up. The stillness, the quiet rustling of tall grasses beyond the fence, soothed him. He nodded for an instant, nearly falling asleep from exhaustion. He hadn't eaten since noon, and he really wasn't in the best of shape for such exertion. *Keep moving; keep moving:* the words repeated meaninglessly in his spinning head.

Behind him, a slight noise. His fatigue fell from him like a cloak. Whirling, he rose, to face—a small insect, tapping singlemindedly at a flake of rust. Steldan's head swam; he drew a deep breath and walked stiffly toward the construction yards. The fence would not stop him—not now.

Soon he was back, hoisting a heavy cylindrical device. The yellow-and-red label, dimly visible in the city light, read: *Type C metal-cutting laser. Primary focus: 5cm. Dangerous to 2 m.* Specifically designed to be useless as a weapon, the searing beam of the bulky tool diverged from focus beyond the two meters; the same was true of Wilth's surgical lasers: they cut flesh cleanly for a centimeter past the wand tip, and were harmless beyond.

Setting the safety goggles over his eyes, Steldan snapped on the power switch and methodically ran the laser back and forth against the fence. Somewhere, alarms went off, loudly announcing the breach; no sound of them reached Steldan. All he heard was the sizzling of molten bond-wire, and the soft hum of the laser. Four minutes later he was through the fence. He paused long enough to stamp out the tiny fire that the beam had touched off in the low, dead-brown grass that swept up to the fence. He ran. Headlong flight, legs working. His fear, his own imaginings, lent him the strength to cross those fields, to free himself by losing himself. If there was any pursuit, he never learned of it, and after half an hour he was a free, if nameless, citizen of the City-South.

Part II
Weeks of Searching

Chief of Naval Operations Admiral Cambrai, although not a young man, rivaled many a wet-nosed teenager in his immaturity. Lean and weathered, with wisps of silver hair straggling from under his cap, the Admiral thought of himself as a wise elder and a knowledgeable leader. His bristling white eyebrows, piercing blue eyes, long, thin nose, and the ancient wood pipe he constantly puffed, gave him a look of inner strength and quiet reserve, an impression he always strove to project.

That he succeeded at all was due primarily to the fact that he could keep his mouth shut.

His intercom buzzed while he was practicing his poker face. Opening the line with a pencil slapped across the switch, he asked brusquely, "Are they here yet, or have you more excuses?"

"They're here, sir," answered the voice of his aide.

"Well, bring 'em in," snapped the Admiral, and he swung his feet off his desk, sitting straight in the chair, resting his arms dignifiedly upon the desk top. The door opened, and the aide entered with a thin file, which he slid carefully onto the Admiral's desk. Saluting, the young man spun and left.

Cambrai slouched back, propped his feet up again, and hooked the file closer with a boot. *I got that boy pretty well trained,* he laughed and, smiling, opened the pages.

First Battle of Binary (it read), 1103 Standard.
Overview:

Under the command of Grand Admiral Rothar Sienne, thirteen capital ships and twenty-eight screening ships moved into action against twenty Sonallan ships of uncertain classification. The Concordat Navy's ships, in standard formation, fired three volleys of long-range missiles, relying upon long-standing Concordat superiority in missile technology. For some reason not yet understood . . .

Blasted report! growled the Admiral. *I was there! I was Captain of the* Essar! *Stinking missiles! They just plain damned blew up.* "For some reason not yet understood," *my leg! Can't* anybody *see through these lies?* He threw the report across the room, then cursed because he'd have to pick it up himself. Damned if he'd let his aide see his human side!

My ship survived, and one or two others. When I got back, I was a hero. And then all hell broke loose.

Admiral Cambrai was a kept man. A tool. And to his intense disgust, he knew it. The Battle of Binary had been a setup, not an accident. Thirty-eight Concordat ships, with full complements, had been murdered. All Admiral Cambrai had to do was not think about it, and his job as Chief of Naval Operations was secure.

Tell a child not to think about green milk, and watch his face. The Admiral, for all his sixty standard years of age, was as much a child as he'd been at eight. He knew damned well who had murdered that fleet.

Two years of this, he groaned. He'd been asked—ordered—to kill three investigations, and he'd watched Admiral Horst sabotage two others. Through it all, the one winner was Admiral Telford. At the Second Battle of Binary, the younger man had led the revenge fleet into a decisive victory over the Sonallans, splintering their fleets and sweeping on to bombard their planets. In three months the army of occupation held Tenh Sonallae, their enemies' homeworld, and Admiral Telford was a Grand Admiral, the Secretary of the Navy.

Binary. A weird region of space. It wasn't named for any twin-star system; those were disgustingly common. The name came from the paired planets orbiting their sickly-orange star: two worlds that were comfortably livable and strategically vital. Cambrai had been at the second battle also. It had been a trap-shooting match. And trap-shooting is all kinds of fun when enemy ships are your pigeons. The *Essar* scored four kills in that four-day battle; Admiral Telford's missiles didn't malfunction, as Sienne's had.

Cambrai rose and switched on some lights against the deepening gloom of evening. His stark red jacket and ice-white pants and trim brought out the white of his hair and the pink of his skin. He strode about on his thin legs, picking up the strewn papers, and as he did so, he couldn't help feeling a pang of fear. It had been too easy, for too long. Sooner or later . . . For now, however, his job was to quash yet another investigation. He forced himself to read the file thoroughly, his mind wandering only occasionally.

At exactly eight the Subsector Investigator Senior from the Judicial Branch was announced. Admiral Cambrai was ready for him. He was not ready for a Concordat Warrant.

"Open my files to you? No material excluded? That's insane!"

The squat investigator, Deacon Anse, smiled spitefully at the Admiral's outburst. Short, thick, muscled like a wrestler, he grappled issues, pinned evidence. Viewing his job as a game spared him the pains that his more serious comrades suffered; viewing it as a personal challenge made it enjoyable. Fixing his bulbous eyes on Cambrai—and well he knew the effect those eyes had on recalcitrants—he hastened to reassure the Admiral, making certain not to reassure him at all.

"I only need to see the files on the missile types at Binary," he leered. When he wanted to, Anse could be thoroughly and appallingly vile.

"You'd have to be an engineer just to read them!" snarled Cambrai. "Listen, boy; you get it in writing exactly what that warrant is to apply to, and then we'll talk."

"The warrant applies to any file in your possession, and I have a full staff of engineers waiting for the ones I want."

Cambrai puffed his pipe furiously, producing a pungent cloud of heavy smoke. He knew this often annoyed unwanted visitors. "Let me see that warrant," he growled.

"If you rip it," grinned Anse through the haze, "I'll have the Justicar draft another. Personally." He passed across the thick document.

"Rip it. Preposterous." Cambrai had indeed thought of it, but only fleetingly. He scanned the warrant, not really seeing it. "Tell the Justicar that I don't recognize this warrant as valid. Too broad and therefore not legal." He looked up and breathed deeply, blowing smoke as if by accident over Anse.

The inspector's eyes narrowed. "That may have been unwise," was all he said. Realizing that, mercifully, the ugly inspector wasn't going to press much further, Cambrai let a tight smile be his reply.

Anse waited a moment more, then rose and walked stiffly to the door. In the doorway he turned and sighed. "Parke at the Secretariat will be unsympathetic, I fear. He may have to pressure Telford for your resignation." He waited, and after a moment nodded, "Good day." The door slid shut behind him.

Cambrai hung his head, acknowledging eventual defeat. In an age of computer micro-files, destroying the records was impossible. Even if he were to bomb the central computer, the duplicates at Sector Headquarters, and on most Concordat planets, would remain. Survival was impossible. There was, however, one last thing he could do to protect himself.

"Get me Admiral Horst," he rapped into his intercom. "I'll need an execution order."

The Improved Dreadnought *Caerleon* hung motionless, massive, white-and-silver, shining against the billion stars. High in a parking orbit above the purple planet Sopenstil, home of the Navy's First Fleet, the ship waited inactive, fusion fires banked low. Bristling with banks of energy cannon, with antennae sitting in clusters upon the hull, and deep missile bays recessed into the armored flanks, the ship was a proud monster even in idleness. The length of it gleamed, tinged lightly red by the sun. The mighty engines thickened the craft's stern.

Aboard a two-man carrier, Commander James Tyler watched the approaching ship sardonically. *Pretty fancy, just for killing people. For myself, I prefer hand grenades.* Beside him a crewman held the controls that brought the shuttle toward the assigned docking port. Soon the monstrous ship swelled, filled half the sky, and absorbed the smaller craft. A row of green lights on the shuttle's control panel indicated that the two craft were linked. The crewman stood, stepped back to the lock, and cycled it, standing aside to let Tyler pass.

Tyler stood, stretched, and exited the lock, then, seized by an impulse, a whim, he turned back to face the crewman. He stood there, silently, his eyes boring into the crewman's face. The crewman waited, motionless, confused. Tyler still stared at him, aiming his eyes just a fraction below those of the crewman. Was this a game? The crewman tensed. ". . . Sir?"

Tyler stared another second, then, without expression, reached up toward the crewman, who rolled his eyes. None of this made sense to him; it was a violation of the orderly sense of discipline that made the Navy safe, sane . . . Tyler pulled the man's cap down over the man's eyes. As he turned and strode off, Tyler pictured the expression on the bewildered ferryman's face.

Cruelty, it seemed, needed no excuse, and was certainly not limited to violence. Tyler revelled in the mental equivalent of cruelty, for the ferryman would always remember the scene, and flinch anew with each recalling.

Tall and thin, Commander Tyler was a handsome man, with fine blond hair and a comfortable, misleading face. His eyes were open, and cheerful, if somewhat forbidding, and his mouth was set in a perpetual grin, reassuring, easy, false.

He strode along the corridors of the *Caerleon,* bringing himself at last to the office currently occupied by Grand Admiral Telford. He entered without knocking.

"Who—?" began Telford, starting up from his desk. Tyler turned a smooth gaze upon the Grand Admiral.

Telford, knowing that courtesies would be wasted

upon this incorrigible, said after a moment, "Sit down."
Tyler sat.

"What brings you here?"

"Oh, Admiral Cambrai asked me to have someone killed. Per your orders, I came to check with you first." The voice was bright, alert.

"Who was to be the victim?"

"Athalos Steldan, on Chirkun."

Telford winced. Steldan. The trouble he'd caused had reached even here, into his headquarters, into his office. His enemies were mobilizing, preparing an offensive to force him from office. Steldan had started it.

Nevertheless, Cambrai's action seemed surprisingly abrupt.

"Why kill him? Horst's organization can easily track him down and capture him."

"Will that keep him silent?" The gray eyes bored into Telford's face.

"Horst can hold him incommunicado. He won't be able to spread any more tales."

"Can you afford to gamble? And what happens when he comes to trial?"

"He's done his damage." Telford seemed uneasy. "What more can he do?"

Tyler said nothing, and gazed at Telford's throat.

"We'll let Horst—" Telford began; Tyler interrupted him.

"He can guide your enemies through another investigation of the two Battles of Binary. He can harass you by releasing documents to the Judiciary or the Secretariat. He could start a small civil war among the bureaucracies merely by pointing out what has already been done to him in the absence of formal charges. He—"

"He ran away before he could be arraigned!"

"Why was Horst given an unlimited budget for capturing one fugitive?"

"That was Cambrai's order, not mine."

"And who pulls *his* strings?"

"Tyler. Listen to me." *How much does this man know? How much?* "I . . . I don't care to discuss Steldan further. If Cambrai asked you to . . . work on Steldan's case . . ." He met Tyler's gaze. "Go ahead." He dropped his eyes. "And don't get caught, all right?"

"Yes, sir. A pleasure, sir." He rose and walked to the door. "Oh, by the way, sir . . ." He grinned widely. "Would you like his ears?"

"Get out!"

"Yes, sir." Tyler strolled insolently from the room, exiting grandly without looking back.

Grand Admiral Scott North Telford, Secretary of the Navy and Commander of the Fleet for the star-spanning Concordat of Archive, was perhaps the most misunderstood officer in the service. Of above-average height, with receding straw-blond hair, his eyes looked out of caverns worn in his face by overwork. Some looked at him and saw a skull, leering in unholy shrewdness. Others saw him as a trustworthy, tired man, infinitely wise and understanding. In truth he was neither, merely a man, like all others, irreducible and complex. He had his faults, and was aware of most of them; he had strengths, and knew how to make use of them.

The offspring of a wealthy, well-placed family, he had begun as an inspector in a support flotilla in the Navy. Earning his commission by luck as much as by skill, he'd pushed his career to the top by hard work, and by taking gambles that he knew were justified.

Tyler will kill Steldan, he knew. But if Tyler were caught, things would become very ugly, very fast. Some of the blame could be shrugged off on Cambrai. Cambrai might be forced to retire, but with his full pensions and benefits, and a slush fund gratuity on top. Telford didn't imagine that Cambrai would mind. Horst could take his place, and pull the pressure away from the Operations Branch, possibly onto Commodore Rudolfs.

Telford closed his eyes, his schemes evaporating under the weight of his cares. *Who's the bigger idiot: Tyler, Cambrai, or me? Which of us is blackmailing which? Tyler has almost as many hooks into me as I have into him.*

Prepare something.

He drafted two letters to First Secretary Parke, who

was at best a neutral in the squabble. He ordered two investigations: one, legitimate, of Rudolfs, and one, a dummy, a sham, of Horst. He knew how to get Cambrai's Vice-Chief, Admiral de la Noue, in charge of the upcoming investigation that Justicar Solme was preparing. The one looking into Admiral Cambrai's activities, was the one Telford felt most concerned about.

De la Noue? She was by no means one of his tools. He had to depend upon her Navy loyalties to keep the investigation harmless.

Was there any way to appease Solme? Probably not. The old Justicar, in combination with that ever-angry Foreign Secretary, Vissenne, had it in for him. Maybe if Vissenne could be so angered that he made some foolish blunder . . .

Telford's future lay on Chirkun, held by Steldan, threatened by Tyler, pursued by Gray. And Steldan had plans of his own.

The Leonidas City-South at the best of times was an ugly holdover from a darker age. Peeling tenements and narrow streets framed crowded marketplaces and weedpatch parks. Here felons had their lair, and the hopeless lay in wait. Athalos Steldan hated it.

He knew enough of the area to avoid its worst dangers, and he was canny enough to survive its subtle perils. He stayed well away from the purple strobe lights of the drug parlors; he held back from the glaring paint of the strutting prostitutes of every sex. He skirted encounters, without appearing to be avoiding anything. Above all, he kept his distance from Wilth and his band.

His plans were half-formed, and still rather hypothetical. Wilth would figure in his eventual schemes, and soon he must be contacted. But as an enemy, ally, or tool? Steldan's cash was holding out well: several weeks' accumulated pay from the brokers. His tactical situation was acceptable; his strategic situation was unpromising. Something would have to give, soon.

None of his plans, however, included discovering his captor, the man he'd been grilled by that day in Wilth's headquarters. It was on his seventh day in the City-South slums that he heard the voice.

The street was crowded; dozens of citizens walked aimlessly, slumped, hangdog. Steldan had long since grown sick of the sameness, of the gray streets and the institutional-tan paint flaking from the monoblock buildings. Around him, the murmur of voices all mingled, merging into a dull background drone.

One voice stood out.

The man who'd held him in anticoncussion ice; the criminal leader. Steldan, walking numbly, knew that within paces of him, unaware, was the underworld leader. Could the knowledge be of use to him? He realized that it could; and quickly rearranged his plans . . .

The voice went on, speaking swiftly, somehow mixing anger and placating plaintiveness at the same time. He was ahead of Steldan, to the left—him: the obese man, triple-chinned, fat-cheeked, head cocked to the left. His hair was short, his clothes baggy and yet clinging to his knees in a ridiculous fashion. Quickly the picture was clear to Steldan, observing and not observed. The tall man to the criminal's left was a hireling or henchman; the three stout bravos near them were a bodyguard corps; and at least three of the casually strolling strangers ranging ahead and behind were bodyguards and scouts.

Continuing forward as if unconcerned, Steldan strained to catch the conversation. He failed, until one of the closer men leaned in and addressed the fat leader as "Mr. Danliffe."

"Danliffe" turned partially, said something indistinguishable in response, and returned to his private conversation. At the nearest public transport station, Steldan fell back and watched the party close ranks and depart. Within minutes the next train arrived, and Steldan was swiftly aboard it, pursuing his former captor.

He nearly missed their exit; just in time he leaped from the open car, having seen a glimpse of one of the trailing bodyguards rounding a corner.

Soon he was in pursuit again. After a long march through the grid of unchanging streets he was rewarded with a view of Danliffe's home. A towering monoblock, the house was seven stories high, and seventy meters broad and deep. A glance at the place as he walked hurriedly by showed it ringed with lounging bodyguards well-disguised as street loafers, but still plain enough to a trained eye. A security viewscreen was inset in the large front door, protected from apathetic vandalism by a clear chain plastic sheet. All the windows were shuttered; the roof shot upwards, steep and without opening. Danliffe and his friend disappeared within.

Hours passed. The bloated sun dropped diagonally toward the opposite rooftops. Blue-black shadows lengthened. The bodyguards began to drift toward the doorway.

At five o'clock exactly, the door swung inward and the tall man, Danliffe's companion, stepped out. In the shadowy interior, Steldan glimpsed Danliffe himself. Three of the bodyguards walked off in formation about the tall man, and a knot of seven loitered at the door for a moment, finally to amble away in two groups.

Steldan followed the visitor, noting for future use the exact address of Danliffe's home.

"Believably clumsy," Danliffe had called Steldan's earlier intelligence work. Danliffe would learn.

Steldan knew the unpleasant fact of life: In a computerized society, privacy remains attainable. Secrecy, however, does not. Any one fact can lead, step by very logical step, to any other. Steldan had the first fact: Danliffe's name and address; and he had access to computer time at the coin-operated "plain-language" reference stations to be found wherever there were public phones.

Four minutes' work, at a cost of two half-credit tokens, gave him the name of Danliffe's visitor: R. Chalcitas, one of Danliffe's junior partners in the false identity business. In five days he'd blown a rift between them.

Beginning at an electronics shop specializing in semilegal phone-fooling devices, he picked up an inexpensive false-coder. Hefting the thing in his hand, seventy grams of molded gray plastic, he admired the many functions it would perform: extravagantly expensive voice-disguising functions and a modicum of timing operations. Exiting the small shop with its thousands of wall-mounted trinkets, Steldan failed to notice the proprietor's careful look of appraisal; he was unaware of the hidden camera that captured his image.

He phoned Danliffe, who clearly had the most characteristic voice Steldan had ever heard. Danliffe's choleric, excitable nature expressed itself, not only in his bluff voice, but in his attitude as top dog: insecure, not far short of paranoid, displaying weaknesses that could be played upon.

"Danliffe?" Steldan asked, the voice-tuning function of the false-coder making another man of him.

"Mister Danliffe to you, whoever you might be." The belligerent response covered the faintest note of agitation.

"And it will be *Mister* Chalcitas you'll be calling your so-called underling, in only a few weeks. Listen . . . Shut up, fiddle-mouth, and listen to me. I'm not doing this for my health, you know?"

Danliffe, fuming, listened. Steldan spun out the story as far as he could, blending generalities, facts, and guesses into a plausible fable of treachery and double-double-dealing.

"Wilth doesn't know what Chalcitas is up to. Not yet. But he's the key to it all. His files, his coders, his verification blanks . . . You see? He's your man, now. But Chalcitas is no dunce; he's got his moves all set. And you're none too free with the rewarding hand."

The call was being traced, Steldan knew; the false-coder made the call seem to originate from Chalcitas' home, from one of the lesser-used numbers on his phone trunk.

"What do you want?"

"You'll get a signal. When you do, be ready to move."

"No. You." Danliffe fished for a clue to his caller's identity. "What do *you* want?"

"We'll talk another time. Listen carefully. The key is Wilth. Without him, Chalcitas' whole scheme falls through. I'm going to give you a keyword."

"Wait! I can trust Wilth. Why should I trust you?"

Steldan was ready for that. "You'll trust me because

you have to. But Wilth? He holds all the files. You need him, but does he need you? Think about it." He rung off.

That was easy enough; another phone call cemented the suspicions in Danliffe's mind. Steldan phoned Chalcitas, false-coding the call to a public phone in a criminal-frequented tavern in the City-South.

"Chalcitas?" The voice Steldan used was that of a drug-crazed denizen of the lowest sort. The sophisticated electronics added the accents and timing for him, leaving mysterious pauses, or jamming the words all together in a rush.

"What?"

"Listen closely: 'Alpha Two Schurrie Total.' Got it?"

Before Chalcitas could say anything of the nature of: "What might all that mean?" Steldan had disconnected. Chalcitas was merely perplexed, but Danliffe's wiretappers saw it differently. Poor simplistic Chalcitas was actually unaware that his line was tapped at all.

And for Wilth, rotten to the core and proud of it, Steldan contrived an almost ideally compromising conversation. This time Steldan's voice was, in seeming, the voice of Danliffe himself. It wouldn't fool anyone who took the time to study the voiceprints; it wouldn't have to. The words that Wilth found himself tricked into saying would indict him in Danliffe's eyes, no matter what the justification.

"Wilth?"

"Mister Danliffe? I don't know if this line is safe."

"I've checked it. I want to talk about this Steldan character."

"He cut and ran. I can't find him. Too bad, too . . ."

"Have the lasers arrived?"

"Five of 'em. Lovely little tools."

"You've lied to me, Wilth." Steldan, impersonating Danliffe, said this calmly. True to his guess, calmness from the ordinarily hotheaded criminal was more frightening to Wilth than open anger would have been.

"I never did," Wilth denied, too hastily.

"You failed to inform me of the Concordat ships in orbit, searching for Steldan."

"I didn't know!" That was true; Steldan remorselessly charged him with the falsehood.

"You failed to inform me of the origin of the lasers: Concordat Navy Medical Branch stocks at Kurgan."

"I didn't know that, either!" Also true; also beside the point. Would Danliffe choose to take a simple denial at face value?

"You failed to inform me that Steldan was of Captain's rank, with Medical Branch training, yet with Commerce Department experience."

That, Steldan knew, was totally unanswerable. Wilth had known those facts, because Steldan had told him. If Wilth had, as it now seemed, failed to mention even one of those facts to Danliffe, then the guilt would automatically carry over to his earlier two accusations.

"Well?" Steldan demanded, driving home the point.

"I'm sorry, sir. I never thought it was important enough to bother you with."

A game try for an evasion. Against the real Danliffe, it would have failed. Steldan, however, chose to accept it.

"Hm. Very well. Don't let this happen again."

Danliffe, himself, reviewing the tape of this conversation, would be intrigued, to say the least. It would seem that Wilth would be asked once again to answer the same three questions. Discord was well sown.

The telephone, Steldan thought, *is one of the finest weapons humanity has yet devised.*

He cautioned himself that this plan would never have worked against a well-led and well-motivated contingent of criminals. Danliffe's gang was not one such. The plan looked more workable each moment.

Communications between the stars were slow, limited to the courier networks that hauled messages at the seemingly brisk rate of fifteen hundred times light speed. Slowed some thirty percent by detours and refueling considerations, the relay system was laid out so that Lieutenant Ron Gray was constantly seven weeks ahead of his latest orders. To ask a question and receive a response took fourteen weeks, delayed another week or two by Sector Headquarters' impossible volume of business. Even a priority one signal couldn't do better than those fourteen weeks.

Accordingly, Lieutenant Gray had been given virtually a blank warrant, with unlimited access to the central Concordat file bank on Chirkun, a limitless expense account, and a free hand. And because of that, Lieutenant Gray soon found himself digging upward as fast as downward. Through strata after strata of obscure references, he pursued the truth. Eventually, he found it.

Athalos Steldan, then a Lieutenant Commander in the Records Division of the Intelligence Branch, had been an administrator, clerk, and inventory control man. He'd been the man who'd ordered the self-destruct frequencies altered on the fleet's missiles at the First Battle of Binary. The evidence was clear. Gray found an account of the battle, a copy of Steldan's assignment order, and his later transfer orders. Finally, searching carefully, he'd found, buried under mountains of trivia, Steldan's scrawled signature, unmistakable, on the inventory control sheet, with his initials by the frequency change notification.

Following a hunch, Gray tracked down a report on the standard Sonallan combat ship. When he found it, he heaved a weary sigh. Their navigation radar was of exactly the same frequency as the Concordat missiles' destruct mechanism.

The missiles had exploded in flight as fast as the Sonallans could track them. The image was almost frightening.

In Gray's mind's eye, a missile bay hung, crash-nets draped against the walls, harshly lit, open to the midnight of open space. A battery of launchers bulked low, gray and angular. With a clank that could be felt the length of the vessel, fifty standard missiles, each twelve meters long, coal-black, stubby-finned, were ejected. They darted forth, grew tails of fire, and homed on their targets. At a safe distance from the launching ship, they armed themselves. Sonallan radar played over them, registering them upon the enemy computers for defensive consideration.

Defenses, however, were not necessary. The missiles exploded, blooming, blossoming, bursting, all harmless incandescence in empty space, nowhere near their intended targets.

No wonder the battle had been lost. Gray's head swam. Why had this been unknown until now? Because he alone had known where to look. Previous investigating bodies had simply been swamped with too much data. Why, then, were they after Steldan? He must have slipped somewhere. By now, someone else had probably duplicated Gray's research, and the two-year-old mystery was already solved. To Gray had fallen the last detail of capturing the saboteur.

The ghost of a doubt surfaced in his mind, only to resubmerge. Something he'd known earlier . . .

Although he was certain that this was old data, he prepared copies of what he'd found, drafted a report of his conclusions, and had it sent uphill to Commander Finch at Subsector Headquarters. That was only a three-week trip, and Finch could see that it got proper attention at Sector. Out of thoroughness, he sent a duplicate of the material to the local station of the Concordat's Judicial Branch.

After that, he set himself to capturing Steldan as quickly as he could.

"Harcourt, have you finished with those forged references yet?"

"No, Lieutenant," she answered wearily. "Since Block 10—"

"I know, I know: 'Files are in a disrupted state and missing records have yet to be reconstructed.' "

"It's the most common response to any computer query, sir, and I'm just as sick of it as you are."

"Oh, well . . . Carry on." Gray massaged his stiff back and shifted his chair. From behind the partition he could hear Harcourt typing in another inquiry, no doubt to receive the same maddening not-quite-answer. On his desk he shuffled the statements of several witnesses who'd known the real Ramo Tiernif. The description they'd given was close enough to Steldan's, but the photograph dispelled any doubt. Steldan had ghoulishly reincarnated a man who had been burned and more than burned. The authentic Ramo Tiernif had been vaporized, atomized, and ionized in the explosion of the *Block 10*.

How had Steldan known the name to choose? How could he have known that Ramo Tiernif was of his build, height, weight, age, and general appearance? Had he interviewed survivors, finding people who'd known a tall, dark-haired dead man?

At the brokers' offices, Arve Brantos Jr. had identified Steldan's photo as that of the man he'd hired, and beside him Arve Brantos Sr. had nodded once, saying nothing, staring fixedly at the flustered Gray. John Bourtzos had been more voluble, giving as many details as he could remember about the new clerk. L. Tempes had glanced at the photo as at a doorknob. Showing no trace of interest, he detailed all his conversations with clerk Tiernif. The four part-time junior clerks filed in in a clump, glanced at the photo, glanced at Tempes, glanced at Bourtzos, and nodded nervously in unison.

Lieutenant Gray had left the offices hurriedly, feeling the senior Brantos' eyes boring through the new blue-glass doors and watching, watching, watching Gray's burning face.

Steldan awoke, groping dizzily. Relaxing, he stared at the dingy gray ceiling of his apartment while the phrases "Theme with variations" and "Explosion!" chased themselves through his mind. It had been good fortune that he found a place as comfortable as this in which to live; scratching in gutters was something he held to be undignified.

Although he found it comfortable, he had yet to discover that it wasn't safe.

From the doorway to the small flat's bathroom, a sweet voice asked, "Are we awake?"

Steldan waited a moment, then slowly turned his head toward the stranger. Lounging comfortably in the doorway was a tall woman in a black one-piece outfit. Large black eyes in an oval face gazed calmly at him; her brown hair hung straight to her shoulders. From her left hand a heavy laser pistol dangled insolently, massive, black, and deadly.

Steldan eyed that pistol. *The size of a small cannon. It really would suffice to come after me with less firepower.*

"On your feet, tough guy. Let's see how brave you are." Her sarcasm, her patronizing tone, seemed totally unnecessary to Steldan.

Deliver me . . . he sighed. "How'd *you* get a bounty-hunter's license?" he sneered. "Seduce the commissioner?"

The gun leaped up; Steldan rolled down off the bed, and launched himself at the woman's knees. She brought the gun-butt down hard, lacking time to aim the weapon. He caught her wrist on his forearm, blocking the clubbing blow. She tried to kick him, lifting her black-booted foot for a crushing smash. He unbalanced and floored her with a quick sideways sweep of his forearm.

She fought, and fought well. Steldan had less skill in the rough and tumble, and was bruised and battered before his advantage in mass and reach settled the issue. Soon she was disarmed, although he gave her enough credit to consider her far from helpless. He caught up the pistol and covered her with it, still holding her pinned beneath him.

"Bastard!" she spat.

"For what it's worth, I apologize for the insult. It was simply the first thing I could think of . . . that would have had that effect."

She refused to respond. Steldan couldn't blame her. At her hip he found the flat pouch with the license: "Linde Volke: Authorized to pursue and capture at own risk Athalos Steldan. Reward promised: 25,000 credits. Signed: Lt. Ron Gray, Concordat Navy." Affixed was a photo of Steldan, and a brief, small-print summary of the applicable laws.

"He's offering that much," he said absently.

"You're sitting on me," Linde said in a measured tone.

"Impolite of me. Sorry." He stood and covered her carefully with the pistol. He hadn't fired one since his routine weapons check-out during advanced training. Holding the heavy device level, he tried to look familiar with it.

"Bastard!" she hissed again, rubbing her wrist.

"You could have phoned Gray and told him I was here. You'd have been rewarded the same. But you came alone. Why?" Rather to his surprise he received an answer. More to his surprise, it was an honest one.

"I needed to prove myself."

"I'm sorry I got in the way." Linde registered surprise; Steldan was not being sarcastic.

"You sound like you mean it," she muttered, looking sidelong at him.

"You wanted to test yourself. My motivations, I'm afraid, are slightly more base: I merely need to escape capture."

"Do motivations determine performance?"

"I've come to believe so. I don't like the idea of testing oneself. It seems to be based upon the presupposition that the testing is needed. The terms of the proposition are negative."

"What do you mean?"

I'm standing here debating psychology with a woman, holding her at gunpoint, he thought ruefully. *Why am I always so dependent on the position of strength?* On the other hand, he doubted that she would listen to him any other way.

"Taking a test implies that unless you pass, you've failed. Black and white. Can you classify a person as a success or as a failure?"

"I've failed so far," she said in frustrated fury. "You've got the gun."

"And with that fool offering twenty-five thousand for me, I'll probably need it." Gesturing with his free hand, he herded her into the closet by the bed and shut her within it. After wedging a chair against the door, he dressed himself as rapidly as possible.

Inside the closet, Linde leaned against the wall and waited. He'd let her out again, she knew. He'd need to ask her about the bounty. She straightened her rumpled skinsuit and brushed back her hair.

"All right," Steldan said warily, moving the chair away. "Come out, slowly, and avoid disconcerting me. I'm armed and you're not."

She complied. "You won't get far, you know."

"Maybe not. However, I can't stay here. Turn around." She spun partway about, and regarded him over her shoulder. Steldan quietly and professionally bound her, tying her arms to her sides with bands of bedsheets. He tied her legs similarly, and cocooned her in two blankets, mindful of her circulation and comfort. Placing her on the bed, he backed off and retrieved the gun.

"Now we'll talk," he stated. Saying nothing, she gazed at him, a disconcerting speculation in her eyes.

"How did you find me?"

Her eyes strayed to the ceiling. "I asked the right questions."

"Give me an example."

"For example, Mister Steldan, you would do well to buy your false-coders on the black market, and not in public shops. I paid only five hundred credits for that roll of film, and yours is the fifth photo."

Steldan frowned. He wouldn't have thought of that. He found himself puzzled by her attitude. At this point he'd expected her to be spitting curses at him, trading him insult for insult.

In any case, he dared not tarry. He bent down and gagged her, checking that she could breathe, and explained quietly, "I'm leaving. With twenty-five kilo-credits over me, there will be about fifty of your type out on the streets. It shouldn't take you over three hours to wriggle yourself free, at which point I suppose you'll take up the chase again. Thanks for the gun."

With that he rose and left the apartment, leaving Linde in the darkened room. She heard his footsteps receding. Her fingers, bound to her legs, began feeling along the fabric of the skinsuit. Soon she found the hard flatness of the razor-sharp blades sewn into the legs. With only a little struggle, she sliced them out of their pockets and sawed the bedsheets away. Jackknifing loose from the blankets, she ran to the door and peered out. Steldan was not in sight.

Imagining herself in his place, she ran to the rear exit of the apartment block, and peered both ways along the outside alleyway. No sign of him was evident.

She closed the door, and retraced her steps for a short

distance. Another door let into a stairway; she grinned to herself and headed down. At the bottom, moving silently, she slipped around a corner and into the access tunnel beneath the building. It ran away slightly, dimly lit by pale orange fluorescents, until a turn cut off her sight. Ahead of her, moving quickly yet carefully, her quarry was visible, ducking around the corner without a backward glance.

Her opinion of him climbed a trifle; she admitted to herself that it was no disgrace to have been captured by him. Although he plainly didn't know this area very well—the tunnel leading in the other direction was a safer route to the streets—he seemed competent, diligent, thorough . . .

Her quarry slipped into a service compartment. She saw, as she pushed her face around the corner, the cover plate closing behind him.

He'll wait there until nightfall, and escape the city by dark, she judged, and softly ran back the way she'd come. Unwilling, she had to approve of his strategies. Too bad for him that she was more clever.

Two hours later, early midmorning, she returned, rearmed now with a new, gleaming black laser pistol. It had taxed her bank draft, but she felt that the heavy pistol, with stunner attachment, gyroscopic reflexes, and photomultiplier gunsight, was an indispensable tool. She pushed the select lever to the stunner function, giving her options she had lacked with her old pistol.

Around the corner, safely hidden, she lounged, waiting.

Inside the dimly red-lit service compartment, Steldan studied the wiring exposed before him until his head swam. Although the conduits, branches, trunks, and colored cables were labeled, he lacked the electronics expertise to identify the codes. One section was probably the telephone and computer line, carrying coded laser pulses over optic links; lacking a headphone-linebreak apparatus, he had no way of eavesdropping on what were certainly uninteresting conversations.

The heavy power cables interested him more, and

presented some appealing possibilities. At the switching post he found a trace diagram, and above him, to the left, a junction box. Using the laser pistol tuned to its cutting function, he carefully severed connections, stopping often to pore over the diagram.

A diversion, he hoped, would aid his escape. What he'd done, or tried to do, was weaken the system just enough that tonight, when the building's tenants turned up heat and lights, the cables would overload and short out. In the darkness, while people gaped in their rooms, he'd have the best chance to sneak away. He'd steal a ground car, maybe even an air car, and head north.

Sorry, people, he apologized silently. *It's this, or lie down and die, and I'm too stubborn, too scared.* He sat with his back to the wall. *When will it all end? I'm not worth CR25,000!*

He peered at the pistol with distaste, and, placing the charging pins into a receptacle in the junction box, soon had it recharged.

Have I had any choice, in any of what I've done? He examined the pistol. It was heavy, bulky, of black metal unrelieved by any color; it was usable as a tool, when set as a cutting laser, or as a weapon. *Here,* with the lever forward, each pull of the trigger sent forth a needle beam of hot light. With the lever depressed and pushed another notch forward, the beam was continuous, cutting anything in front of it for as long as the trigger was pulled.

What sort of person was Linde, that she preferred such a weapon? How, he wondered, could he hope to understand such a person. At the surface, she seemed to be simple and easily categorized; beneath that he had sensed currents of . . . dependence? Fear? She seemed unlike anyone he'd ever known before, yet wholly and wholesomely familiar.

I swore I'd never trust anyone. Is that a livable life? He felt that in Linde he'd sensed a need . . .

But I'll never meet her again, will I?

He looked again at the weapon. In medical school he'd seen hospitalized victims of laser fire; their veins seared shut, muscles and tissues sealed by the beam into black, cracked crusts on top of angrily secreting raw flesh . . . "A merciful weapon," the instructor had said, not believing it any more than the students. "Had these patients been shot with slug-throwers, over half of them would be dead by now." Steldan had been the assistant at the amputation of the left leg of a graying Marine Colonel. He remembered the man cursing quietly . . .

Steldan drained the pistol, and, after some effort, cracked the oscillator fiber, effectively destroying the weapon. He left it on top of the wiring junction box.

What, softness? From the man who betrayed Sienne's fleet to the Sonallans? He smiled. At this point, he could be crippled in a dashing rescue of a thousand trapped schoolchildren, and it wouldn't save him. Shooting a couple of bounty hunters wouldn't even be read into the charges.

The Marine Colonel had given him a cigar, he remembered.

Near the hour of sunset he awoke from the catnap he'd fallen into. He sat up, groped about, and quickly pulled himself into alertness. He lay on the floor of the small basement service compartment. Reaching out, he could feel the heat emitted by the weakened power cables. He opened the small access plate and was stunned by the wave of hot air that gusted out. The conduits were melting, quietly fusing themselves to the metal frame of the cabinet.

In less than ten minutes, the wires shorted across, burning out with a small explosion of bright sparks. Glaring light arced, then darkness flooded in. Instantly, Steldan threw the door-plate wide and entered the dark hallway. He had no way of knowing how much of the building he'd left without power; with luck he could get to a parked car.

"You lose, friend," called a woman's voice from behind him. It was Linde. A low-power stun beam hummed from her gun, boring into Steldan's shoulder, toppling him. With her new gunsight, she could see perfectly in the dark. Steldan fell back into the service compartment, and pulled the door-plate partway closed behind him. His shoulder and right arm refused to obey him, and only with difficulty was he able to scramble fully into the small cubicle. Trapped . . .

Another stun beam hummed out of the dark, causing the metal door-plate to vibrate unpleasantly. For a moment he regretted destroying the laser—and realized that Linde couldn't know that he had.

"I'm armed," he shouted, "and won't hesitate to fire."

"But you can't see me, can you?" Linde jeered.

"With a gun like this, does that matter?" His only reply from her was another stun shot, which transferred its energy harmlessly into the metal door. *This can't last long,* Steldan knew. The ruined circuit would show on the power system's central telltales, and it couldn't be more than a few minutes until a serviceman arrived to repair it. Or, more likely, another bounty hunter, guessing the meaning of the power outage.

"My friends will be here any minute," he lied. "There's a telephone circuit in here." It sounded forced and hysterical even to him; Linde made no answer. In the smothering darkness she crawled forward, trying to line up a clear shot at the compartment. Soon she lay in a hollow space in the wall, her head near the half-open door-plate enclosing Steldan's hiding place. She was safe from him; her only problem was to close in and stun him, preferably before others of her profession arrived.

Steldan, hunched tightly in the corner of the compartment, massaged his right shoulder, trying to rub feeling back into his stunned nerves. Sitting quietly, he chanced to hear the scrape of cloth upon the floor, and knew that his hunter was closing with him.

"No closer," he called.

Linde, in her niche, heard his voice only a few meters from her; through the photomultiplier she saw the hallway as empty.

Blast! How do I get him out of that closet?

She saw no way to winkle her quarry out of his small fortress; she didn't want to give her position away by speaking. The tense stalemate stood unchanged for some time, each of the pair frantically thinking of ways to end it. Steldan, in his unrelieved darkness, felt the passage of time keenly, knowing that soon it would be too late.

Soon it was.

Linde first heard the approach of a third person along the hallway. The stranger carefully edged nearer, out of sight behind a further bend in the passage. With her nightscope Linde could see nothing, yet she remained certain that she was no longer alone with her quarry.

With no warning, a thin red lightning bolt flashed, illuminating the hallway for a split-second, splattering off a wall. Darkness fell again, confused by sparkling green afterimages. Steldan, in the service compartment, felt the heat of its passage; it had been aimed at Linde, but seemed to have missed her. Another beam glanced along the hallway, for a moment clearly showing the details of wall and ceiling. Again darkness fell, leaving afterimages dancing in his vision and in Linde's.

In the brief flash, Steldan had seen her, exposed in the passage, shielded partway by his half-opened doorplate, yet still dangerously unprotected. He kicked the door-plate open wider, offering momentary armor against the trigger-happy assailant's beams. "In here," he called to her.

"What?" she called back, disconcerted but not panicked.

"Get in here, before you're fried," Steldan hissed.

Linde scrambled through the door, skewed about in the cubicle, and sighted through her nightscope. Snapping off three low-buzzing stun-shots of her own, she ducked back. "One of them, all right." She spoke carelessly to Steldan beside her. "He's mad to be firing fullpower laser shots. It's a violation of his license." She seemed at ease in the near presence of her enemy, yet slightly chilled by the trigger-happiness of the hunter outside. All her attention was focused out the now fully open door-plate.

By this time the stun effect had completely worn off Steldan's shoulder; he was free for action, but with no way to jump. If Linde was comfortable with him, he was quite nervous with her this near him and yet unseen. A shot cut through the darkness, showing him Linde lying on the floor, observing the hallway through her scope.

"We're trapped," she announced quietly. "He's alone, but he's got the hall covered." She couldn't predict what would happen; the situation was not one covered by her ideas of tests. She had reasoned far enough ahead to realize that the man at the end of the corridor needed them dead, to prevent them from reporting his illegal actions. Such callousness appalled Linde, who was not able to operate at that cynical a level.

"Set up a diversion," Steldan urged, and his voice soothed her nerves.

"How?"

"Under a barrage of rapid fire, we could leap while he pulls back."

Linde stopped, thought, and in the dark bent over her pistol, adjusting the automatic firing switches by feel. Placing the pistol flat on its side on the floor of the hallway, she pulled the trigger, releasing a hailstorm of bright red bolts skating down the hall.

Steldan leaped first, followed by Linde. Together they ran frantically down the hallway, ducking soon around the corner. Linde's pistol continued to fire pointlessly, two shots per second, toward the unseen enemy. The shots were returned; in the flickering scarlet illumination given off by the sharp discharges, the hallway was fairly well strobe-lit. A dim figure hung just behind the far corner, barely visible. Any minute the man would discern the ruse; perhaps he already had.

"It's a shame to lose that pistol," Linde griped. At that moment its power-pack died, and the last three shots feebly glowed out, more and more dim. The gun was dead, the hall dark.

"Come on," Linde urged. She knew that the bounty hunter pursuing them would be moving cautiously toward them already.

Steldan weighed his responses briefly, and leaped back into the hall, dashing the few meters to the pistol. He grasped it, wincing slightly at its heat, and ran back to the corner. He reached safety just as a brace of glue grenades burst, filling the hall behind him with a stringy foam of adhesive filaments. The sharp stench, acrid and chemical, of the air-drying glue made his head swim. None of it had touched him, however; he and Linde ran down the cross-hall. They burst through another access door, and were soon out in the cool evening air, striding rapidly along a back alley.

"He can't come the way we did," Linde judged; "he blocked the corridor against himself with the glue. But he won't take long to find his way up here . . ." She set out briskly toward the alleymouth. Steldan jogged beside her, watching her closely lest she remember his worth.

Planets can be as varied as people, he thought, *and cities even more; back alleys are civilization's one great constant.* With a pang, he looked up, and scanned the high buildings on either side. *Rooftops, too: ambushers love 'em.*

What is she thinking? Aloud, he asked, "Where are we headed?"

"I know a safe place."

"Where's that?"

"My apartment. Small, but safe."

Steldan swallowed his objections and continued running. Soon they came to a side street, lit but dimly by decaying orange-sputtering street lights. Linde cast about, located a parked ground car, and quickly had it open. Steldan ran an unhappy eye over the dented yellow length of it, and at the way the whole thing listed slightly to its left. Without attracting undue attention, Linde disconnected the interlock and engaged the engine. With Seldan safely inside, she slid the ill-tuned contraption into the street. She handled the relic with skill, following the web of streets that was the City-South.

"I suppose we can dump this thing at mid-town," Steldan suggested thoughtfully, perched nervously on the passenger's seat. "We'll ride the tram to the New City, and double back by slidewalk."

She looked at him with a questioning expression. "You trust me?"

"I—" Steldan began. *Do I?* "I will, for a time. As long as you're with me, you can't inform on me, can you?"

"I could scream for a policeman."

"Why don't you?"

Her pose broke down. "It would be a betrayal. After being through that firefight together, after you helped me escape, do you think I could do that to you?"

"That kind of money can numb a lot of conscience."

"Do you think that's all . . ." she snapped, then subsided. In a few minutes she pulled the ground car toward a curb and disabled its controls. She leaped out and threw back the power-cowl.

"Recharge the pistol from the accumulator," she ordered.

"I prefer it empty," Steldan said matter-of-factly. Linde glared, then turned and marched away through the nearby gate to the tram station. Steldan stuffed the huge pistol in his belt and followed. Inside the substation they caught the next line to the rebuilt Leonidas New City.

After a few minutes of silence, Linde asked, "What do they want you for, anyway?"

"Sabotage. Military sabotage."

"You're kidding!" She drew back, until, ashamed of her unease, she sat down again. "Did you really do it?"

"No."

"But you'd say that anyway."

"And I ran, which supposedly is an admission of guilt."

"You could have been framed?"

Steldan looked at her. His expression softened. How did she see him? She wasn't looking at a murderer, or a saboteur; she was looking at a strong man chased by a pack of curs. The sense of adventure was filling her at the thought of the hunt. Suddenly Steldan realized that, strong woman though she was, she remained quite childlike in her viewpoint.

"Framed? Yes, actually, I was. The important thing is that I get away."

"Why? Would they kill you?"

"I doubt I'd even be given a trial. They'd shoot me and dump the mess in the nearest furnace."

"Then they were lying about the twenty-five thousand credits?"

Careful, Steldan cautioned himself. "No, that's real.

But they've got it to spend. Their budget for stopping me comes from the combined slush funds of half a dozen services. Oh, they'll take their time to pay, with some tricky surcharges, waived on the receipt of certain guarantees . . ." *Translated freely, I just said that I'm the good guy, and they're the bad guys. Have I ever played other than fast and loose with the truth?*

"It doesn't matter," Linde exclaimed. "I believe you, that you're innocent. And I can help you, I think."

Steldan couldn't afford to turn her down. Following the formula he felt would most sway her, he promised: "When I've proven my innocence, I'll remember your help. Thank you." He felt like an unprincipled bastard.

"All right. What should we do for now?"

I was hoping you'd suggest a course. "We'll continue with the plan we've got so far: lose pursuit and then hide. After that, I have some tools worth using. I've still got a fair deal of cash left, and we can use it—"

"To hide in comfort?"

"No," he said carefully. "To counterattack."

"How much have you got?"

"No twenty-five thousand, that's for sure. We'll just have to stretch what there is. Have you got a safe phone line?"

"No. It's not guarded."

"First thing we'll do is install a guard-circuit, with my false-coder—"

"I've already retrieved the false-coder you had at your apartment. I did that when I bought the new pistol."

Steldan nodded. "With it, all our phone calls will appear to come from another part of the city."

"What does that gain us?"

"Free phone service, for one thing."

She turned to see the flippant grin on his face; he had more in mind, and wasn't ready to speak of it.

Soon the train stopped at the Central City Station, unloading its small group of passengers. Steldan led Linde to the lower-level slidewalk terminus, and chose a line toward the City-South. Although the service did not extend beyond the New City reconstruction area, this was a fast way to double back on their trail. Few people were on the swiftly sliding path, and in the illuminated tunnel, Steldan could watch for followers.

The slide broke the surface at the Ravine Station, the moving rubbery material of the way easing them gently yet insistently to the right of the speedlane. Beneath the moonless night sky, the two passed the terminal shops, threading through the light evening traffic. From there they ascended a ramp to street level. They stood near the uncertain boundary between the New City and the City-South; the buildings here were new, freshly faced with plate-stone, glimmering white beneath the stars. A few blocks farther south the old architecture prevailed, with the newer, taller buildings giving way to squat megacomplexes of five and six stories.

Subtler details were the smaller windowspaces of the older complexes, and the flush columns along walls for piping and wiring trunks. A spirit of modular centrality, of prefabricated and prestressed, space-filling design was common. These and other details reflected the pressing lack of resources that the city endured shortly after its founding. Colony worlds nearly always passed through this stage; Chirkun had escaped the pattern earlier than most due to the disastrous Block 10 explosion.

Linde conducted Steldan to a third-level apartment in a large, anonymous complex, and led him in through a securely triple-locked door. Inside were comfortable, if worn, furnishings: a couch-chair-desk combination in a deep blue, and a well-stocked computer and library tucked neatly in the corner.

"Well, what do you think?" she asked, a trifle defensively.

"It looks remarkably personable," Steldan answered her, gazing about. On the walls were sand-paintings, delightful works of swirling grace in brilliant reds against tan, fixed permanently with transparent plastic. On several shelves were candlesticks, shards of ancient tile, and a substantial hourglass collection. The home was personalized, unique. Steldan, having lived his entire life in institutionalized housing, felt a brief pang of regret.

People shape and are shaped by their homes, he knew; this one bespoke a happy and basically healthy owner.

"Well, sit down," Linde muttered. "This will be your home for a while . . ." She seemed ill at ease; more was bothering her than the break in her normal daily pattern.

"Thank you. I shall be scant bother." Steldan sat gingerly, while Linde went off to produce bedding. Again, he was struck by the association between the apartment and the occupant. The small three-room flat held her scent, her warmth. He, by being here, was as much an intruder invited as he would be as a trespasser. Plainly, he'd be forced to watch his behavior at all times. After a while, perhaps, she'd be comfortable with him. Until then . . .

Soon she had him settled, with a bed made of the couch and a cleared space in a corner for his belongings. At present these were no more than the clothes on his back. With a polite flourish he returned to her the pistol.

They spoke for some time, elliptically and fragmentarily, of past experiences. Steldan, to his startlement, found himself opening up to her; he clasped an icy grip of control over his heart.

". . . I didn't stay with the trade," Linde said, her eyes focused on a distant memory. "The darned machines were putting the grooves into the metal, and it was just for me to supervise. But what supervision is necessary on an automated flat-lathe?"

She shook her head, and recalled herself: "Here I am reminiscing about my old jobs; you must find this unexciting. I never meant to bore you."

"You aren't." And that was true. The cadence of her words soothed him, yet stirred, deep within him, a turmoil that he kept buried only with difficulty. *I've known her less than fifteen hours,* he thought, *and nevertheless, I trust her. I'll sleep in her home, at her mercy. Perhaps I'm merely tired of running.*

They sat close to one another upon the soft-carpeted floor. Linde looked down, never quite meeting Steldan's gaze. The silence stretched out, with its message abundantly clear. Loneliness was the message. Steldan sensed this at last, and closed his eyes. He took his emotions in his mind and he wiped them, scoured them, killed them. He hardened his heart; he murdered his feelings before they could become truly part of him.

Aloud, all he said was: "We should probably retire. Tomorrow will begin our challenge."

Linde looked up, frowning very slightly. Her thoughts, which had been wandering, dissipated, the dreamlike zephyrs of her idle reverie now lost forever. She almost wished . . .

"Yes," she smiled. "Tomorrow."

Steldan smiled, and turned away. Linde looked at his smile, and it still seemed false. Before retiring, she recharged the pistol from a wall plate, and rested it beside her bed. She carefully locked her door, and slept the night with a light on.

"What do you mean, 'we're losing ground?' " Lieutenant Gray demanded.

"It's true," Harcourt replied blandly. "Computer simulation shows an increasing number of places he could be, and a decreasing probability of our catching him within any fixed amount of time." She paused for breath, but nevertheless overrode Gray's attempt to interrupt her. "His probability density function is still the heaviest in the City-South, with peaks in the least savory sections, and the Spaceport still reads clear, but the ninety-nine percent contour is expanding at three percent per day, with uncertainty parameters fluctuating wildly."

"And by all of this you mean . . . ?"

She looked up from her papers and stared at Gray blankly. "Just what I said." She turned and disappeared behind the room divider, toward her cubicle. Gray closed his eyes. Harcourt stuck her head over the divider and said, "In very simple language, what it means is that we don't know where he is."

"Thank you, Harcourt," Gray sighed. "And stop standing on the chairs."

"Yessir." She disappeared again, to apply herself to her computers.

Gray returned his attention to his desk where his day's agenda waited, as prepared by Harcourt.

1) Follow-up on Bounty Hunters.
2) Appointment at noon with C.I.B. subchief Lance. Cancelled yesterday by Lance.
3) Report via Courier to Sector H.Q. on progress: urgent. Have prepared by 12:15 deadline. Your head not mine.

Gray rolled his eyes to the ceiling, then resumed reading the list.

4) Summarize all progress to date: "By wallowing in the obvious, new insights may be had," your quote.
5) Check with Scouts on low-orbit patrol.
6) Take Harcourt to dinner.

Gray suppressed a sigh, and mechanically crossed out the last entry. The report from the Police Commissioner on the Bounty Hunters had been routine, with no progress and no claims. He'd expected nothing from C.I.B. subchief Lance anyway, and was more relieved than disappointed by the cancellation. And his report to his superiors was already with the messenger, headed for the Courier station across the Spaceport. He'd agonized over that report, trying to express optimism when it seemed he'd pretty badly dropped the ball.

Let's wallow in the obvious, then, he decided.

On his large yellow note pad he wrote, in a clearly legible block print, his thoughts as they came to him.

"Point one: He's had help. His falsified documents, retrieved from the files at Brantos, Brantos, and Bourtzos, were of professional quality and expertly composed so as to lull the suspicions of prospective employers. While he could have done the composing, he would have been unable to do the printing involved.

"Point two: As an Intelligence Officer from Records Division, he can be counted on to make no mistakes as to organization or record-keeping. On the other hand, lacking field experience, if he makes a mistake, it will be one of action, not of planning.

"Point three . . ." His hand, almost of its own will, set

down the pen. There was nothing to be gained from this effort.

"Lieutenant Gray?" called Harcourt.

"Yes?"

"I've been thinking," she said, and stuck her head over the partition again. "You've been relying too much on paperwork and computer searches. I thought, well, why not follow his path directly? We know where the pilot dropped him, out in the parklands, and we're pretty sure of how he got to the city . . .

"Why not send a guy out to go underground, as if for real, following Steldan's route as exactly as possible?"

"That would be admitting that a quick end to this hunt isn't forthcoming."

"Is it? We've been chipping away for two months now, and things are getting worse . . . Now if one of your Navy underlings were to go out and dig in for real, and try to hide from you while staying in the city, he'd be more likely than you to bump into Steldan accidentally."

Gray's mind swam with objections. "Your C.I.B. certainly has undercover operatives, doesn't it?"

"They don't tend to live very long," Harcourt said, her mouth firmly set.

Gray understood enough to keep quiet about that. "What about the bounty hunters?" His private misgivings about the use of such mercenaries were best rethought in the light of Harcourt's explanation. *Undercover men are chosen to be the best; how could any small, local group of criminals best them?*

"The bounty hunters?" Harcourt sneered. "They aren't hiding, they're hunting. That makes all the difference. If one of your men were to try to bury himself . . ."

"For one thing, I don't have any men attached to me. Now, I could have one assigned to me by the portmaster, but . . ."

"It's the only way."

"It would be so uncertain."

"It could also help plug up holes he might need to use in the future. Furthermore, it would help my department by rounding up the clowns that rigged his identification." Her voice dropped a little. "Maybe if you helped us, we'd be more enthusiastic about helping you." Gray glared at her. "No, not me!" she hastily asserted. "People like Lance, or some of the other subchiefs."

"It would take a long time."

"If you saw these computer simulations, you'd be in less of a hurry." She sped on, before Gray could object. "The guy who'd try this—or maybe two, or more—"

"One would be enough," Gray suggested. "Two people on this trail would be dangerously redundant."

Harcourt nodded, and proceeded at a slower pace. "We'd do it double-blind. We should actually not know where he is at any time, and he'd know this, but he'd have an implanted transponder to locate him at need, and he'd know that, too."

"Double-blind? Why . . . ?" Gray scowled.

"It'd have to be that anyway. He couldn't keep us updated on every change of plan. Rather, he'd have to be free to react to the situation." She leaned her arms on the room divider, delivering her ideas as if she stood before a podium, not upon a chair.

"We can alter the police patrol patterns—you've got that authority, the gods know how—so as to channel Steldan and our man together, perhaps—"

"All right," Gray decided abruptly. "You've sold me. I'll do it."

"Who do we send?"

"Harcourt, you're not listening. *I'll* do it."

"You?" Harcourt asked in shock.

"I've got the field experience, and despite what you might think of me, I *can* drop the Navy mannerisms at need. What's more, I can do my own forgery, with damned little equipment."

"But who'll run this end of the show?"

"You will, of course. You know my routine as well as I do; maybe better."

"Steldan's seen you!" she objected. "He'd recognize you, and—"

"Wrong. He did *not* see me. I was in another room when he fell through the ceiling." He thought for a moment. "No, he couldn't possibly have gotten any kind of a look at me."

"I'll call the C.I.B. armory; you'll need a pistol."

"No, I'll pick up an illicit weapon in the City-South. Steldan started with nothing, and so will I."

"How good a shot are you?"

"At the firing-range, 96.2. In combat"—he grinned—"somewhat better."

"I think you're going to enjoy this," she said, eyeing him sidelong.

He looked at her appraisingly for a moment, then suggested, "Why don't we discuss that over dinner?"

In three days the plans were completed. Gray would be given a two-hour head start, and then Harcourt would call in a warrant for his capture for questioning. Every police captain in the city would know that this was only a test, but the patrolmen would treat it as real. Precautions were taken so that no one would be injured, and Gray intended to surrender peacefully if he had no reasonable route of escape. Primarily, however, this was to be a battle of wits, with him attempting to escape attention as much as capture.

"I've got a low-level capture order prepared," Harcourt informed him as he readied himself.

"Don't waste too much manpower on me," Gray reminded her again. "Keep trying to find Steldan, as you have been."

"I still don't see why *you* have to go; we could send any number of your Navy subordinates."

"We agreed on this two days ago. I'm the closest to Steldan in terms of training, experience, and expertise. Further, one field agent is enough; two would be too many. I'll keep in touch."

"Good luck, Ron."

He waved, and left the office, walking calmly as if to an appointment with an underling, not the underworld. Striding the Spaceport promenade, he felt the subtle thrill of the hunted man, and hiding places were apparent to him that he'd never thought of before. His three weeks in Naval Intelligence School survival class came to mind: when he and thirty other trainees were to escape from simulated enemy patrols on a desert world a hundred light years from here. He remembered the blazing blue sun, the pale sand, and orange rocks. He'd been among the last captured, he recalled proudly, although his escape from the "prison camp" had been an abortive fiasco. The principles were the same, with different dimensions. There, visibility meant line-of-sight; here it was a function of behavior. There, escape meant head-down, flat-out running, throwing oneself behind barriers; here, it was more important to carve out boltholes ahead of time, to have prepared escape routes that were not always physical paths.

Ten minutes had elapsed. It was time to put his plans into effect, although he had only sketched them out. He left the Spaceport by the main underground slideway, heading south. At a cross-path shopping mall he stopped and found a cheap clothier. Soon, he'd switched his work uniform for a set of nondescript street clothes. Twenty-five minutes had elapsed. He ascended to street level and caught the tram to the City-South station.

There he transferred to the next train back to the downtown station, situated nearly eleven kilometers from the Spaceport. Next he took the slidewalk back beneath the streets—paralleling Steldan's and Linde's path, had he but known— to a point near the City-South junction.

One hour left. Walking the gaudied streets of the City-South slums, he searched for the type of drinking and drugging establishment that would best serve his purpose. It was early evening, and the street lights were blinking on, casting into shadow the niches and holes where the lowest forms of vice were sold. Glaring lights had been erected, advertising food, drink, weapons, gambling. Coded lights, purple, green, eye-hurting white, promised prostitutes, hallucinogens, pain-for-hire, and other esoteric services—some so vile that even Gray couldn't think of them without grimacing. After twenty minutes of walking back and forth along one street (during which time he knew he'd been spotted by lookouts and catalogued as a mark), he pushed his hat into his pocket and turned abruptly through the doorway of a drug bar.

The paths of humanity are tortuous, but they are negotiable. Cultures vary wildly; their constants are immutable. In the dimness, virtually blind, Gray felt the gut-wrenching fear that outsiders must feel when invading a tightly closed society. Further, there was a sense, entirely in his own mind, of contrast, of meeting. He was a straight-living, clean-minded person, a cog in a rigidly efficient and logical machine; the inhabitants of the bar were tired, hungry men and cruel, weary women, lost forever to the virtues that Gray held dearest.

He stood motionless in the entrance, while cold eyes sized him up, while lookouts signaled masters, while a hundred powerful scents tugged at his nostrils. His eyes adjusted to the pulsing red glow of the interior. He stalked in, as if angry, and took a chair at an untenanted table. Hallucinogenic vapors tinted the air: euphorics, depressants, offworld steams, alien mists.

Unprepared, Gray would have been lost in mere seconds, succumbing to a green dream, a delirium of sexual metaphors from which he might never have awoken. As a field officer in Concordat Naval Intelligence, he had been immunized to such psychotropic drugs, and while his head remained clear, this only heightened his sense of two alien cultures in conflict.

The striking snake of logic; the web-spinning spider of the occult—was he indeed beginning to hallucinate? The image of the two creatures remained with him for a moment. With a shrug, he snarled for service. The sounds of speech were muted in this place, and he knew he was being watched. Cold eyes were upon him, spiders' eyes . . . A large man loomed up, coldly tossed down a doughy mass onto the table, and retreated through the fogs. Gray recognized the lump as a vacuum fungus, grown in kilns locally, and advertised as "imported from deep space."

Perfect, he judged. It couldn't affect him, although they'd deliberately given him enough to kill ten addicts. He looked awkwardly at the lump, and pulled off two fingers-full. Cramming this into his mouth with feigned appetite, he nearly gagged on the rancid oiliness of the vile semifluid. He spat it onto the floor, swept the rest of the spoiled drug after it, and called for better, adding three or four choice curses.

"Sorry," said the large man, returning with a bottle of gray liquid. "Took ya for a newbie." Gray glared at him, then grinned crookedly.

"I've been away. Passing through."

"Need work?"

"Yeah. Something. Anything."

"Drink yer sterco, then talk t' me."

Gray scowled. "All right." He ripped the top off the bottle and drank deeply. This, too, he was immune to, and the flavor was much better. After a few minutes, during which the other man watched him closely, he drew himself to his feet, rubbed his jaw, and approached the vendor. They studied each other for a while, Gray faking mild dizziness, turmoil.

"What did ya think?"

"I've had worse."

Gray noticed that the other customers in the bar were carefully looking elsewhere.

"What're ya good at?" the man asked; Gray did not pretend to misunderstand.

"Engraving. Engrav—" He frowned. He smiled. "Been on Gooderlle, a ways away. The idiots use paper money."

Regarding Gray intently for a moment, the man seemed somehow less dangerous, to be as gullible as anyone else. In an eyeblink, Gray's illusion of a different society with a different mode of thought collapsed. The room was still dark and filthy, but it seemed to him that more light seeped in than before. He took fresh stock of the decor: the dark metal inlay of the floor, the scarred wood walls, the once-lustrous bar. He felt the gut-level relief that outsiders must feel when accepted into a tightly closed society.

"Go to the Orina down the street, to th' left. Ask for Wilth. He'll know how to use ya." With a small, sketchy gesture of support, the man turned away. Gray stood for a moment, then departed. The fresh air of the street was almost painfully invigorating; the street noises came to him as a small hurricane of confusion after the stuffy silence of the drug bar.

He found the Orina without difficulty, and entered it without hesitation. Much like the place he'd just left, it stank of the foul concoctions sold there, and once again it was only Gray's immunity treatments that prevented him from losing his sanity to the fumes.

He cornered a sharp-eyed thug behind a counter and asked bluntly, "Where can I find Wilth?"

The thin-faced man stared at Gray for some time, his face alternately hidden and revealed by the pulsing scarlet glow of the room's centerpiece. Gray thought absently about the exact calibration of the color and frequency required to produce the maximum subliminal effect. Probably subsonics were also broadcast, and certainly those and other weapons waited, ready to be used against invaders. The subtle poisons of the room floated through Gray's midbrain, leaving no trace.

"You the engraver?" the man asked at last. Gray nodded. "The guy from the other place called ahead. Got any of your work on you?"

"Um, no," Gray admitted. "I can prove myself, though."

"C'mon upstairs." Gray followed him through a curtained alcove and up a flight of stairs lit by ancient blue glow-plates. He recognized these as standard colonial stock, dating from the first settlement of Chirkun, some four centuries past. So long a time, for the world to have advanced so little.

He was shown a door by his guide, who turned and left. Gray tapped twice. After a while the door flipped open, and he was invited in by a short, fat man in an ink-stained apron.

"Wilth'll be right with you," the gentleman said, and gestured Gray to enter. Inside the long, low room were five large drafting tables and a photoreproducer press stocked with standard printing templates including electronic security coding setup. Here, Gray decided, was the best-organized forgery lab he'd ever seen; infiltrating it became, to him, a truly rewarding pleasure.

Wilth came up to him shortly, and Gray was shocked by the gauntness of the tall figure. The pale face and sunken cheeks spoke of stress and of turmoil. Gray also suspected that the man had been partaking of the drugs available downstairs, despite the fact that drug merchants, more than anyone else, knew the idiocy of doing so.

"What can I do for you?" Wilth asked, a sneer taking any politeness out of his words.

"Well, I've had some experience at this kind of setup, and I think I can help you."

"Do you know how to run these things?" Wilth asked, gesturing toward the cameras, presses, and electronic coders.

"I've had a fair deal of practice."

"Then to start with, turn out an I.D. card for yourself. Phillip here will help you." Both men knew what Phillip would actually be doing: watching Gray carefully, judging him. "I've got a spare name here, that you can use . . . You will be William George Douglas, age 36, birthday 254-1071 . . ." He rattled off the series and registration numbers. Gray copied it all carefully on a piece of scrap paper lying on the nearest drafting table.

"He died in the Block 10 explosion," Wilth continued, "and we got his master file. Ask Phillip for I.D. blanks."

In three hours Gray had punched out an I.D. card in the name of William Douglas, with his own photograph attached, and an electronic coding fiber that authenticated the card for any scanning devices. For the time being, Gray was effectively Douglas. Wilth had not asked for his correct name, which surprised Gray; he'd had a cover story already planned in great detail.

Phillip, the fat printer, expressed approval for the job, pointing out a flaw in the location on the card of the series number, but approving the work as fully acceptable. "Paper money, you say? On Gooderlle? I'm going to have to see about visiting there . . ." Gray looked forward to turning in this band of forgers. No doubt the C.I.B. would have collected them in time, although with the colossal confusions left in the wake of the explosion, the normally efficient agency was stretched to its limit. And the forgers had proven themselves adept at fighting back.

Wilth had apparently left word with the shop's bodyguards that Gray was not to be allowed to leave until he'd been thoroughly cleared. The large guards apologetically helped Gray bed down for the night in the soon-deserted printing room, and one of them stood watch while Gray slept.

In the morning he was given a lengthy interview with Wilth.

"So, Mr. Douglas. Do you like it here?"

"Yes. You've a damned well-stocked shop, and I'll be glad to work here."

"You understand that you're still to be watched for a while. It's not that I don't trust you, but I don't need to take chances just now."

"I see. What should I start doing?"

"We'll begin you with I.D. cards. Everyone in my organization should have at least two, and I'd like about seven."

"All right. When do I get paid, and when will you trust me enough to let me go?"

"For now you'll room upstairs," Wilth answered evasively.

And when I am let free, thought Gray, *I'll be carefully followed and watched, until they fully trust me.*

"You'll be working with Phillip—he's the shop boss," Wilth continued. "Right now I'll need you to turn out some special card blanks. Something with a glitch in the coding fiber that will trigger a security scanner. It should guarantee that the bearer will be arrested."

"That'll be easy," Gray said slowly, thinking it over. "We can put an actual physical kink in the fiber. That's something we have to be careful about anyway."

"Good. Hammer out about twenty, and leave 'em with Phillip. He'll take it from there. For now, sit down"—he gestured toward a pair of small straight-backed chairs—"and tell me about yourself. Where do you come from?"

"I was born in Actinius City, on Glame," Gray began, glad at last to be able to use his carefully prepared story. "I picked up photoprinting on Morana, in a government printing office during my first term of universal service. When I thought I'd learned enough, I left. Tracing one person through the blasted Concordat is next to impossible"—how well he knew that to be true—"and since then I've been working at odd forgery jobs."

Actually, Gray had learned forgery techniques in Naval Intelligence School, and had practiced little since then. Fortunately, he retained his hand, and was capable of turning out as good an I.D. card as anyone in the building, save maybe Phillip.

Wilth listened attentively, accepting the story uncritically. "All right, then. It's good to have you. Things will be slow for a while; we're having trouble"—his face twisted a moment with frustration—"but we'll be on good footing inside two weeks."

After a few more minutes of discussion, Wilth took his leave of Gray and left the shop. *We're having troubles indeed!* he thought, and took the front elevator to the street. *That blasted maniac Tiernif. If I'd known he was worth CR 25,000, I'd have turned him in myself.* Tiernif was uppermost on his mind—Tiernif whom he knew to be, in fact, Athalos Steldan.

I wonder what the Navy wants him for? I wonder what I can get out of this?

It was Steldan—it had to be—who had ruined his working relationship with his boss, Danliffe. That was the only explanation that made sense. Danliffe, however, felt that another explanation was more likely true: that Wilth, Chalcitas, and half a dozen others were involved in plotting revolt. Danliffe knew that only luck had put him in charge of the organization; Danliffe knew that each and every one of his underlings was more qualified in useful and practical skills than he was.

Wilth's protestations of loyalty went unheeded. Danliffe chose to believe that he was being undercut. And the belief, combined with the actions it drove him to, were turning the delusion into a reality, in the best tradition of the self-fulfilling prophecy. Wilth and Chalcitas *were* loyal, and would have remained so, had Danliffe only returned their trust. Without it, though . . .

One of the kinked-fiber I.D. cards was carefully being fitted with a name and a photo: Danliffe's.

* * *

At the offices of Brantos, Brantos, and Bourtzos, the three partners were doing their best to make Harcourt feel uncomfortable. They sat in a solid line facing her, while clerks in the background scurried quietly as mice. Arve Brantos Sr. stared relentlessly into Harcourt's face, as did his son. John Bourtzos would gaze at the ceiling, then the floor, only to snap his gaze suddenly toward his guest; his speaking voice was clipped, harsh.

Harcourt was having none of this.

"Steldan was with your firm for twelve weeks?" she asked carefully.

"Yes," snapped Bourtzos.

"And he gave you no cause for mistrust?"

"None."

"What exactly were his duties?"

"We've been over this before. Files and price searches. Check-out bids. Client relations."

"Could he have made purchases or changed procedures without your knowledge?"

"No."

"Yes." Senior clerk L. Tempes moved easily into the room, gesturing a vague deference to his masters, a different ghost of a bow to Harcourt, and then standing silently. After a moment, Harcourt was moved to ask: "How?"

"By using the personal verification coder that Mr. Bourtzos has upon his desk."

"But . . ." Arve Brantos Jr. sputtered. "That would mean walking in and looting the desk—like a common criminal!"

"Steldan? Common?" Harcourt smiled. "Not recently."

"But to use my coder without my permission . . ." Bourtzos scowled furiously. Harcourt decided that new ground was being covered, and congratulated herself for thinking of the follow-up visit.

"The coder: may I see it?"

The Brantoses stared at her, one inimical, placid, attentive, silent, the other with furrowed-brow hostility. Bourtzos hesitated, then flicked a hand toward Tempes, who disappeared quietly. He returned after a moment and handed Harcourt a small gray box, brought from Bourtzos' office. She examined it for a moment, and handed it back to Tempes with an expression of disgust.

"It's nothing more than a coded filament. No identity check; no mnemonic cipher; nothing. Why not just use a rubber stamp?"

"Now listen here—" the younger Brantos burst out, then restrained himself. A tense moment of silence followed.

"This office has always been run with the principles of personal integrity foremost," Tempes said calmly. "If we did not trust our junior clerks, we should soon fall from our exalted position in the business community."

"This time, you got bitten."

"Agreed."

Harcourt looked around the room, taking in the soft blues of its upholstery, the light woods used for trim, and the office machinery atop desks and tables. "May I see the computer files that Steldan had access to?"

Bourtzos and Arve Brantos Jr. simultaneously started to object, only to subside as quickly. "It can't hurt," suggested Brantos, and gave Tempes a nod.

"This way, ma'am." Tempes stiffly led her to a desk top terminal, and rapidly tapped in the security identification.

It took her no longer than four minutes to find the coded order that Steldan had left, causing the files to erase some previous order. In two more minutes she found the acknowledgment of the previous order, and the verification coder's imprint. From there she was unable to progress.

"Mr. Tempes," she asked of the senior clerk who'd stood by her side as she worked, "could I get a printout of all your transmissions for the date 094-1105, say from four o'clock to eight?"

He returned her gaze. "As well to ask for the contents of Bourtzos' private safe. However, I'll convey your request." He stepped out of the cubicle, returning shortly with a firm denial from Bourtzos. "Our transmissions that evening were of a somewhat sensitive nature."

"Oh. I understand." She stood, and headed for the

blue-glass doors. In the waiting room, the Brantoses still sat, the younger whispering to the elder.

"I'll be back tomorrow, about this time," she announced, drawing sharp glances from the pair and from Bourtzos, who was endeavoring to regain his customary grin. "I'll have a Concordat warrant with me," she smiled. Bourtzos' face fell.

"And by the way," she said, just before leaving, "your computer filing system is at least twelve years out of date. Would you like the name of a good software firm?"

Receiving no answer, she departed, amused by the stiff hyperformality of the three partners and their senior clerk.

Weightlifting. That's what they should take up. It'd help them unwind. That, or maybe mountain climbing.

When she returned to her office one flight down, she found Commander James Tyler waiting for her.

Tyler and his aide Rolle approached the looming planet Chirkun in the small, fast spaceship they'd never bothered to name. After they'd been given clearance to land, Lieutenant Rolle threw in the automatics, and the ship slid down the gravitic chute toward the Spaceport's landing grid. They traveled under their real names, safe due to the sheer volume of the Concordat. Not even computers could trace all the billions of people in the irregular sphere; often the best alias a man could use was his true name.

They watched the two scoutships weaving tirelessly over the planet's orbits, blockading the Spaceport against the exit of that scoundrel Steldan. Tyler was impressed, although he tried not to show it. A good pilot could slip past the two Serpent-class ships, but he would need a hell of a good ship, in finest tune. And Steldan was not a pilot.

Neither am I, though, Tyler thought wistfully. Although quite dexterous, his agility was not in the top five percent required for admittance to flight school. He almost envied Rolle, who was a first-rate pilot and a demon in a fast boat. Rolle fumed at the idiotic regulations controlling close-orbit space about Chirkun. He could easily have landed the ship himself, but was forced to sit idle while mindless computers took the controls from him.

Rolle stayed with the ship, intending personally to oversee its unloading and refueling. Tyler gave him a cheery wave and departed. After the formalities at the Portmaster's office, it took him only minutes to find the office shared by Gray and Harcourt. But the room was deserted. He frowned, and picked the lock; he'd only been waiting for ten minutes when Harcourt arrived.

She opened the door and stopped, startled for an instant. Then, critically, she and Tyler examined each other. She took in the black uniform, white pants, ostentatious sidearm, and the air of insolence about the man; he saw a competent, charming young woman, quick on the uptake, and probably faster with the repartee.

"You've probably got the wrong office." Harcourt finally smiled. "We're too big to be chasing mere burglars."

"I am Commander James Tyler, Concordat Naval Intelligence. I've been sent to check up on the pursuit of Athalos Steldan."

"I'm Harcourt, C.I.B. Is a Commander bigger than a Lieutenant?"

"Yes. A good deal bigger."

"Oh, heck. Lieutenant Gray is out on the hunt, and I can't get in touch with him. On the other hand, I've got about fifteen memos that need signing. Would you like to take care of that?"

Tyler let that pass. "I'd like to see a summary of your progress here. I assume you've been preparing such summaries to send to Subsector Headquarters?"

"Oh, sure. Sit there at Gray's desk, and I'll have the computer copy the appropriate report for you."

Half an hour later, Tyler had been brought up to date on Gray's past efforts and current adventure. He honestly couldn't blame Gray for losing Steldan in the brokerage offices, although the trap had been nearly perfect. Gray seemed competent, even allowing for the fact that these reports were tailored for his superiors at Subsector central.

Gray's current scheme, Tyler decided, was the ideal

setup that he himself needed; working undercover with the same double-blind conditions, he would have little difficulty murdering Steldan without being blamed. The other possibility was that Gray or some third party could capture Steldan, forcing Tyler to kill him while in custody.

I can trust Rolle to do that, he judged.

"Harcourt?"

"Yes?" Her head appeared above the room divider.

"I've decided upon my plan of action. I approve of what Gray is trying to do, and I intend to parallel his course."

"He wouldn't like that. Not only would the duplication of effort be wasteful, but he doesn't know you, what you look like, or anything about what you'd be doing."

"I can explore in a different direction than he would."

"But neither of us knows what direction he *is* exploring."

Tyler shot her a glare. "Do you know what I could be doing instead, that doesn't waste my time?"

Harcourt looked to the ceiling. "Filling out blank Navy warrants; drawing upon the unlimited treasury draft; working with the C.I.B.; clearing the reports from frustrated bounty hunters, and giving the commissioner the abstracts; filling out the weekly progress report to send to Navy Sector headquarters—"

"I could grow very tired of you, very fast," Tyler snarled.

Harcourt brightened. "That's the nicest thing you could have said. It makes me feel loved. Either take over here, or scram." She dropped to the floor behind the partition and set to her computers.

Tyler considered accepting this, and decided against it. Savoring his anger as he would a fine wine, he rapped out orders in precise, clipped syllables. "I am in charge here. Under conventions, I take command from Lieutenant Gray. My aide, Lieutenant Rolle, senior to Lieutenant Gray, will remain here with you."

Harcourt's head appeared again above the partition, a bemused expression on her face. Tyler continued.

"I will take to the field in pursuit of the criminal, Athalos Steldan. Any order I give you or Rolle, or that

Rolle gives you, will be followed without question." His eyes were bright, staring fixedly at Harcourt. His heart pounded, and each breath was full and sweet.

Harcourt gazed at him with interest for a few seconds, then asked sweetly: "Did you enjoy all that?"

Tyler couldn't help himself; he broke into a huge grin. "Yes, damn it."

"I thought so. You were good at it. You're also cute when you're angry."

Damndest conversation I've ever had. "Thank you."

"Well, since you've got the rank . . . why not? Call Rolle, and we'll set up a routine."

Rolle, when he saw Tyler next on the communication link in the spaceship, wondered at the liveliness in his boss's expression. Tyler seemed aware, awake. The notion worried Rolle; when Tyler was this cheerful he had usually just killed someone.

By the time Rolle arrived at the Spaceport offices, Tyler appeared normal again, and the callous Lieutenant felt relief. Harcourt greeted the small man warmly, and within minutes they were deep in an animated discussion of computer search routines.

Feeling almost jealous, Tyler made his preparations. In less than an hour he left for the City-South.

Admiral Cambrai paced somberly in his plush office, striding the room's length and returning. His eyes gleamed beneath his white brows as he thought again about the many exquisite tortures he'd like to apply to that damned Steldan. He could watch, and laugh, while someone—Tyler, maybe—applied a neural stimulator to Steldan's spine. That would be satisfying.

He spun about and kicked the desk. Tyler would kill Steldan painfully, to be sure, but Cambrai would never get the full satisfaction. It was too late anyway. Tyler should have reported by now, shouldn't he?

Cambrai sat and fiddled with the computer, getting from it a flight plan from Sopenstil to Chirkun. Guessing at Tyler's top speed—and it would likely be absurdly high, judging by the man's insane pilot—he tried to find a time of arrival. Tyler was almost certainly there by now. When would his coded message arrive signifying Steldan's death?

He rose and resumed pacing. Tyler had gone to Telford after leaving him; he knew from the delicate shift toward disfavor he'd undergone in Telford's view. He was no longer given access to the best operatives, and the lines of communication were subtly being closed. Telford had no use for a man who tended to act in unseemly haste.

It was worse. Anse and his gang of investigators were yapping at his heels, like mongrel curs surrounding a great stag and trying to bring it down. He rather liked the analogy; it helped him bring things back to their proper perspective. Anse and his pack were not likely to get Admiral Cambrai without a bitter fight. He could give as good as he got. He could dish it out. He'd go to Telford for protection.

He decided to have the evidence doctored, just in case.

"How to phrase it?" he wondered aloud. "You can't just say: 'Clerk, erase all references to the Battles of Binary.'" People would talk. Better to have a computer expert, one of his trusted staff, do it. He might know how to do it gently, untraceably.

He sat again and punched the button on his intercom. It would work. It would.

Anse would be in for a nasty surprise.

Secretary Telford completed his review of the First Fleet of the Concordat of Archive. The thick file, printed out by the *Caerleon's* central computer, listed every major ship in the fleet, and minor ships in groups of five or fifteen. The fleet was in excellent shape. Readiness was high; supplies and stores were more than adequate; the perimeter patrols were alert. If the Concordat was surrounded by dozens of potentially hostile civilizations, it was nevertheless the largest and most influential government known.

It was also slowly decaying, Telford knew. He had long since been convinced of the validity of the cyclical theory of civilization. But were the great cycles predestined? He believed not. Decay could be stopped, even reversed. Expansion was not the answer, as it had been for virtually the entire history of the race. The answer was *intensification,* dedicating all of the race's effort to excellence. The Fleet had been dominant for decades because of missile and radar tracking technology. Similar emphasis in areas of economy, shipping, production, and in virtually all other aspects of the Concordat's doing, would guarantee that the present form of government would never fall.

To drive the cold winter away: that was what Telford saw as his primary duty.

Civilizations rise and fall in cycles. But the pattern is not inescapable. Sufficient energy expended at the right time can turn that cycle back upon itself. He put aside such ethnocentrically nonsensical terms as: "It's time they respected us," or "We can beat them at their own game." He was knowledgeable enough to disdain the appeal to the vague enemy known only as "they." He had no use for jingoism. He simply wanted the Concordat to set its considerable will toward improving its condition.

The Fleet was a shambles, literally, when I took over. If Sienne had continued on his ill-conceived course, entire complexes of frontier Sectors would be unstable by now. What has happened has been necessary.

And now people intended to take apart the structure. They wanted to remove the Concordat's best hope: its Fleet.

He knew how to counter them. Sending assassins like Tyler didn't appeal to him, yet he knew that a leader who never uses foul means, only fair, soon is replaced by someone who doesn't suffer from such abstract scruples. Obstructing the course of investigations also worked that way. Was anyone fool enough to believe that Parke, Solme, and especially Vissenne, didn't have assassins of their own? Certainly it was obvious that Vissenne was ordering investigations into the Naval Operations department to hurt the Fleet, and not for any sense of justice.

Vissenne, Secretary of the Foreign Service, officially controlled the Intelligence Service. Nevertheless, Telford had his own Naval Intelligence branch. As far as that went, the Marshal of the Marine Force, although subordinate to Telford, had his own Intelligence branch. Each of them had assassins in their ranks; probably each of them had used them.

He stretched, yawned, and punched for coffee. With a smile of satisfaction he tucked the Fleet Readiness file into a drawer where it would be copied and filed, and the papers blanked for reuse.

Now wouldn't it be nice if we could find a way to read blanked sheets of paper! He thought he had a research team working on that, but it would be a good idea to have Horst check up on it. It certainly didn't matter; he'd always believed that one should never put on paper anything one wouldn't enjoy seeing read by the entire cosmos. The safe file is the one in your head.

He knew that he'd have to make peace overtures to Cambrai; he knew he'd better find a way to placate Solme, infuriate Vissenne beyond logic, and get Parke on his side. Somehow, things didn't seem as bad as they had a while ago. He felt that he'd pull through all right.

He'd just be careful, that's all.

Deacon Anse sat in the well-lit library microfiles room, deep within the Judicial Branch annex on Sopenstil. He hunched forward in his chair, scanning the display screen before him. His large hands fumbled with the keyboard, and he squinted at the black type crawling across the amber screen. He searched for the hidden data he knew was there.

Admiral Cambrai, that afternoon, had received him civilly enough, considering the opinion each held of the other. His expression alternately scowling and pleading, the Admiral had handed across the data-plate, reluctantly and yet without a fight. Not even he could argue with a Concordat warrant signed by Justicar Solme and First Secretary Parke. The old Admiral, however, seemed obscurely confident, as if the file could not possibly contain incriminating material.

Personalities, Anse thought with a sour grin. Foreign Secretary Vissenne hated Admiral Telford as he'd hated no one since the late First Secretary Todut. Solme followed Vissenne, if hesitantly, because the two were the only Centralists in the Praesidium. Parke clumsily followed Solme's lead, for fear of the damage the Justicar could do if angered.

And Telford had his fleet. He could be pushed only so far before he would use it. Perhaps at first he would simply de-emphasize the Naval Base at Vulpina, crippling their economy, or promise Welpern and not Anfor the new shipyards. He was known to be good at sabre rattling; perhaps he would order a general fleet alert, or wargame maneuvers. Long before it came to actually using the fleet for battle maneuvers, the Praesidium would have backed down completely.

The trick, Anse knew, was to undercut Telford's support within the Fleet itself. And that meant Cambrai, Horst, and some others had to be neutralized. Anse's first target was Cambrai.

He shifted in the chair and peered afresh into the display. Page after page of data rolled by, controlled by his typed instructions. Indices were what he most sought, although even they held very few clues to the exact file he desired.

From the planet Chirkun a message had worked its way up, passing through the ranks of the Judiciary Branch. From an obscure investigating lieutenant it had been handed eventually to one of Solme's aides, who saw its value and shot it to Anse.

Athalos Steldan, a Captain in Navy files, a physician, a glorified clerk, had meant nothing to Anse until now. With the message from Chirkun, the name became important.

The computer scanned for the triple data-point: Steldan/Missiles/Battles of Binary. Within seconds the reply flashed: None. Anse scowled. He shifted the search to a copy of the Personnel records, checking for the double-point: Battles of Binary Stocks/Steldan. None. Had Cambrai slipped him an edited copy? If so, why his anguish?

He checked again the message from the Lieutenant on Chirkun. It claimed that missile destruct frequencies aboard all ships at the First Battle of Binary had been changed. Once again he had the computer search for the proper listing in the index.

POSSIBLE appeared in the "results" space.

"?" he typed; "Missile Procedures, Standard," came the reply. "Battle of Binary, Fleet Support, Missile Supply, Miscellaneous."

Anse understood. Computerized filing, with its involutions, cross-references, validation subchecks, and other detailed procedures, made it virtually impossible to delete all mentions of a specific entry. Doubtless Cambrai had tried; likely as not the order for the erasure was buried in the file. Cambrai's tenseness was explained.

Anse kneaded his thick knuckles. Could the record be a sham? Gingerly, he entered the instruction asking for the named file.

The file was no sham.

He read through it, sifting the facts from the mass of trivia surrounding them. There were three entries that particularly interested him. First, the specific order that Lieutenant Gray had found on Chirkun, signed by Steldan and dooming Sienne's fleet. Second, a query from Telford, undated, asked for missile strengths. And third, the transfer order that got Steldan off Sienne's flagship before the battle.

That was intriguing in its ambiguous, yet weighty, implications. It had been countermanded by Admiral Horst, but by the time that update had arrived, Sienne's fleet had departed upon its disastrous voyage. Steldan had lived, but his escape had been a matter of only days. Was it an attempt to murder an accomplice? Or to dispose of an innocent tool? Perhaps neither. Perhaps.

Horst. Anse knew less than he would have liked about the man. As Chief of Naval Intelligence, Horst had more power than Anse approved of. Yet he kept a low profile. Probably he was one of Telford's tools; again, things were too uncertain.

It was Anse's move. He punched for paper copies for each of the suspicious files (and watched with amusement as this fact was appended to each). Carrying them to a composition desk nearby in the library, he spread them out and set to drafting a report, which would be read by Justicar Solme alone. *Alone?* he thought, still amused. The report would be microfiled, security-tagged, indexed, cross-indexed, and someday, maybe, would be dialed by someone investigating some totally unrelated case.

For posterity, then! Anse laughed, and proceeded to phrase the report accusingly.

Admiral de la Noue was an attractive blonde woman of just over average height. She wore her red tunic proudly, representing Cambrai's Operations Branch; her rank-chips gleamed upon her breast.

People often looked into her striking hazel eyes without realizing that an intelligent person looked back. Looked back, and observed. She was young for her rank, and often wondered whether people had over- or underestimated her.

She stood, waiting, just outside the door to the Plenary Chamber, high in the Government Tower Complex, far above the surface of the world that was Archive. The corridor down which she cast occasional glances stretched away, softly lit, plushly carpeted in gentle browns and tans. At the far end, tiny windows let the wan daylight spill in.

Along that corridor, the six members of the Praesidium would soon approach. Already the anticipation ran high among the people waiting here.

At the limits of sight, they appeared: Six men whose ownership of the Concordat of Archive was oligarchic and unshakable. The crowds of functionaries—clerks, guards, officers of the various branches—melted back before their advance. Now and again, someone would edge deferentially forward, impart his or her parcel of information to the passing members, and move back. Tension was palpable, for today's meeting was certain to be unpleasant.

They neared. De la Noue saw Raymond Parke, First Secretary, pasty-faced, jittery, walking just behind Justicar Leonard Solme. The Justicar, senior to them all, stalked ramrod-straight, rail-thin, his sharp face averted from Foreign Secretary Antonin Vissenne. The Foreign Secretary, who would have been handsome were it not for his perpetual expression of seething anger, marched pace for pace with Solme, never letting it be clear who led and who followed.

They neared, and their servants cleared the way for them. Telford, straight and stiff in his gleaming Grand Admiral's uniform, held slightly aloof, walking to one side. He stopped for a moment to confer with a Naval attaché—de la Noue could not see who—then moved to catch up. Behind him, bringing up the rear, were Commerce Secretary Adrian Redmond and Treasury Secretary James Wallace. Liked by all, these two had correspondingly little power. To the degree that they belonged to no faction, and that their deciding votes were earnestly sought, it was strange that they commanded so little prestige.

The final rank of attendant personnel gave way before the advance of the Praesidium of Archive; de la Noue alone stood to face them. She wondered for a moment what would happen if she were to hold her ground. The image of the resulting confrontation was unpleasant, vaguely unsettling. Without further thought, she backed away to her left, and fell into the parade of officials.

The lot filed into the spacious Plenary Chamber, low, wood-paneled, with enough comfortable seating for all. De la Noue found a high seat in the rising bank of amphitheater chairs under the flat dome of the roof, with a view down upon the circular table where the Praesidium sat to debate. Telford's back was to her, with Solme and Parke to the left, the others arrayed to the right, so that Redmond, affable, red hair drifting from beneath his cap, faced her direction.

Six members waited, and behind each was a backup post, where six clerks, Praesidium aides, waited also. Beyond the carved wood of the encircling rail, some fifty spectators watched.

"We're all here," Parke said, needlessly. Vissenne gazed at the ceiling. Wallace's mouth twitched.

"The meeting is now in session." He looked about. "We've got a lot to cover, so . . ." Resignedly, he gestured at the first item on his agenda.

" 'Naval Missile Discipline, with regard to Failure of

Thermonuclear Warheads.' Secretary Vissenne, would you care to . . . ?"

Vissenne nodded, and let the silence stretch out.

"Our war hero," he said at last, "survivor of one-sided battles, by no coincidence the Secretary of the Navy, has several thermonuclear warheads at his disposal. Several. He has proven his ability to use them, and use them to theoretically good purpose. He has proven himself not at all loath to use them. Certainly there are any number of widows and wounded on Tenh Sonallae — "

He anticipated Solme's interruption by spreading his hands and bowing his head, so that the Justicar's point of order was rendered slightly ridiculous in appearance.

"You needn't let irrelevancies slip into your speech, Secretary Vissenne." Solme's voice was low, vibrant, carrying. His eyes flashed. Parke watched him thoughtfully.

"Agreed. I needn't. Admiral Telford's record speaks for itself. I have no need to call additional attention to his actions.

"My business here is as follows: I am not satisfied with the Navy's on-file standing orders for the use of thermonuclear warheads. I have several pressing questions, that I would very much like answered, and, based upon the answers, I have a motion to put forward."

"Proceed," Parke said, and looked away.

"Grand Admiral. How many thermonuclear warheads do you have, and of what yield?"

Telford, who until now had been listening dispassionately, lifted his head and turned Vissenne an indifferent glance. "In fifteen Naval Divisions, across one hundred and fifty Sectors, I have one billion, six hundred and fifty million. These range from half-kiloton tactical land warfare devices to orbital bombardment weapons with a yield of three to five gigatons."

"Planetbusters?"

"That's what they're called in the popular literature. As you're aware, they have no such exaggerated function."

"I see. And for fleet engagements?"

"We use what has come to be called the Standard Missile. Yield equals ten kilotons."

De la Noue, from her seat in the gallery, nodded to herself, thoroughly familiar with the weapon. It was the most deadly thing in space; it was the Navy's guaranteed superiority.

"So small?" Vissenne murmured, sarcasm barely hidden by his gentle voice.

"So accurate," Telford responded, facing him at last.

A silence fell, while they took the measure of one another.

"These missiles. They win battles for you?"

"They have."

"Why did they fail Grand Admiral Rothar Sienne at First Binary?"

"I don't know."

"You don't? I certainly don't. Does anyone?"

"No."

"Admiral, I don't like mysteries. You've had two years to solve this one. I'm interested in hearing your excuses."

Telford took a deep breath. "Secretary, I don't like mysteries any more than you do. There are two reasons for my having so far failed to find a solution. First, whatever material evidence there may have been to work from was destroyed, either in the two Battles of Binary, or in the bombardment of Tenh Sonallae. Second, when I took over the Navy, it was an absolute, unparalleled mess. Files were not only misplaced, files were nonexistent. Stockpiles had been fictionalized, and stockpile inspectors had been criminally negligent. Entire flotillas were undercomplemented. I had to deal with absenteeism, corruption, misfeasance, malfeasance, and nonfeasance."

"You speak very freely and disrespectfully of the late hero, Grand Admiral Rothar Sienne. Are you blaming everything upon your predecessor?" Vissenne's question was smooth, the suavity belied by his bright eyes.

"Sienne was a dotard. I feel no qualms about reviling his performance in office, nor about remarking upon his personal flaws, where they were reflected in his negligence. As for my blaming my failures upon his, that was not my intention. I've succeeded in cleaning out the largest portion of the corruption he let accumulate. I don't see myself as having failed. I merely cannot be everywhere at once, and two-year-old mysteries are relatively low in importance."

"Strong language. And it's handy, isn't it, to have a dead man to blame things upon? Never mind. I'll come to the point." This last was just in time to forestall another objection from Solme. "Neither of us likes a mystery. Perhaps we'll never know what happened to the missing planet of Voss Sector. Perhaps we'll never solve the Bhotian Nebula problem.

"But I think that the confusion surrounding the circumstances of First Binary is something we can dispel. I think a solution is within our grasp. Some ground has already been covered. Were you aware that two other investigations into the matter were called for—apparently by yourself—and cancelled, both times by your Admiral Cambrai?"

Telford nodded. "Yes. The investigating boards found that they didn't have enough data to proceed."

"I would say that more data has surfaced." Vissenne smiled, a smile with no joy in it. "I find, in a table of your upper echelon organization, one Commodore Rudolfs, and one Captain Steldan. Tell me about them."

De la Noue was unable to see Telford's expression. Justicar Solme, however, gave him back an expression so stern and forbidding that it clearly dispelled any hope of succor he may have sought there. Telford turned back to Vissenne.

"Rudolfs is in prison, on charges of selling military secrets. Steldan is currently at large, although we're seeking him on the same charges."

"Trouble in your records division?"

"In every division, Secretary. Records boasts neither my best nor my worst personnel. I invite you to investigate the Naval Office of Industrial Relations."

Vissenne was clearly champing at the bit, ready to press forward. De la Noue never saw what signal that Solme gave him. The result, however, was clear. Vissenne sighed, and his shoulders drooped slightly. His brow unclouded, and with a neutral, businesslike expression, he answered, "I would like to, someday. I think I'd enjoy that a great deal."

He took a deep breath. "I am not prepared at this time, however, to ask for an inquisition. I've made no secret of my dislike for the Navy. Perhaps, as a peacemaker, I cannot bring myself to fully trust the military. Any branch of government that wields a billion and a half nuclear warheads, by definition sets itself in opposition to the negotiation and compromise process. Settlement by reconciliation had always seemed more important to me than settlement by force.

"Considering my prejudices, then, and following the advice of my seniors on the Praesidium, I propose the following:

"A board of inquiry will be convened, to consist of ten Naval officers to be chosen by yourself, and ten officers of the Court of the Supreme Judiciary, to be chosen by Justicar Solme." He paused, looked at Solme, and continued unwillingly.

"The committee will have relevance solely to crimes *per se*—as opposed to derelictions of duty—in the Navy Records Division, and other departments directly related. Only actions discovered to have taken place prior to the conclusion of the Sonallan War are to be covered. The board may recess, but it shall not be dismissed until it returns a real report."

It wasn't what he wanted; it was, however, the most he would get.

Telford, shoulders straight, head high, said, in a low voice: "The committee will be chaired by Admiral de la Noue, of the Operations Branch. She shall have no vote upon the board."

Vissenne's eyes flared. "By no means! If you're offering that as an amendment—" He broke off. Solme, across the table from him, gazed upon him with an expression so stonily remote, so implacable, that Vissenne's words dried up in his throat.

In the gallery, Admiral de la Noue watched carefully, her face stiff. The meeting had suddenly lost its impersonality; her future, her career, were now directly involved.

How well does Telford know me? We've spoken so very seldom. I don't deal with him. Cambrai is plainly a fool; Telford is not, not in the least.

Vissenne broke his gaze away from Solme's only by looking down. His eyes upon his hands, he muttered, "Shall we vote upon it?"

The amendment passed. Should the committee be empowered to investigate the matter, de la Noue would chair it.

"Is there any further discussion?" Parke asked, his voice almost cheerful, as if the interplay of between-Branch rivalries had passed totally over his head.

Vissenne snapped, "Unless the Grand Admiral has something to hide . . ."

"Secretary Vissenne." Solme's warning evidently took Vissenne by surprise; his darting glare was quick and venomous.

Parke watched through narrowed eyes. Wallace and Redmond, flanking Vissenne and holding themselves away from him, were very much spectators to the squabbling. They did, however, pay alert attention. Wallace watched closely, following the emotional by-play, while Redmond took notes upon a yellow pad, recording his impressions rather than the words. The transcribing secretary, behind Parke, took down the words; Redmond took down the facts.

"The vote," Vissenne said at last.

Solme shifted in his seat, looking sternly to his left where Parke fidgeted. "In favor?" the latter asked awkwardly.

Solme, Vissenne, and, reluctantly, Parke himself each raised a hand.

"Against?"

Telford raised his hand, and, to de la Noue's surprise, so did Wallace and Redmond. She was unable to discern their reasoning. It didn't matter. Parke's position as First Secretary carried with it the powerful additional vote, so that the motion carried four to three.

"Is Admiral de la Noue in the audience?" Parke asked, although he knew full well that she was.

She stood, straightening her uniform, and descended the steps to approach the railing. In silence she received the charge of the investigating committee. Solme's secretary passed her an already-prepared list of his choice of members. At the top of the list was Deacon Anse's name.

Telford, turning in his chair, said only, "I'll have ten names for you tomorrow."

They looked at one another. Each now held the other's future. They were bound together by duty. And yet de la Noue's charge came from the Praesidium, not from Telford.

She saluted him, arm stiff across her breast, horizontal, palm down. Telford smiled, a relaxed, accepting smile. Then he turned back to the table, leaving de la Noue to make her exit.

Danliffe slowly lost control of his criminal organization. Piece by piece, the structure fell apart. The obese man felt mingled fear and anger, and frustration seethed behind his florid face. Someone was informing on his men, someone who knew far too much, and the frighteningly efficient planetary Central Intelligence Bureau was picking them off.

He knew, now, who was doing it. If only he'd listened to Wilth in time! He was being undone by Athalos Steldan, the Navy man he'd placed with the shipping brokers. Steldan's lies had been seen through by the planetary government, and they were after him with every trick at their disposal. But for some reason, instead of fighting them, he was attacking Danliffe. Strange. Perverse. Danliffe's man Wilth, in charge of the forgery ring, had been carefully spared. While Danliffe's Slayer Squad had been destroyed, and the hundred small-time rackets under his control were being chewed into, Wilth was actually expanding.

There was only one possible explanation. Wilth planned to take over. Danliffe frowned, staring at the photographs on his desk. Friends of his, all of them, and all but Wilth were now in prison, incommunicado, doomed. One by one he picked up the pictures, setting them aside. Wilth's he pulled from its gilt frame and tore it to shreds in a spasm of fury.

I'm helpless! he agonized. *Only with an opportunity*

like Block 10 could I ever have started. His enforcement brigade emasculated, his henchmen gone, there was very little he could do. And to fail would mean his death also.

He leaped up with an excess of energy, paced twice around his plush room, and sat down panting. Shaking like a leaf, he reached out and fumbled with the phone. He dialed, punching the numbers with a savageness that betrayed his fright. The connection was made, and in a panic he slammed the receiver into the cradle. He'd forgotten to activate the false-coding. The call could have been traced to him, and to this place. Even in extremity, he refused to be that stupid. Modern electronics, he was aware, could trace a call in microseconds, and only the best false-coders could combat this.

More carefully he activated the small device, gave it the location of a public phone on the Spaceport Promenade, and again dialed the number.

"Leonidas City Police. May I help you?"

"Yes. There"—he almost choked—"there is a printing and counterfeiting shop. It's on the second floor, behind the Orina. City-South. Drug shop. I—" He stopped, unable to continue. He disconnected.

For revenge, lacking any other way to strike back, he had as good as slashed off his right arm. It was not the first act of extreme cowardice Danliffe had performed; it would not be the last.

It confused people's plans immeasurably.

Danliffe, defeated, snatched up his hat and coat and bolted. In a sudden flurry of panic he discarded all of his many false I.D. cards save for one, newly made for him by Wilth, updating an alias of which he was particularly fond. Escape—eventually off-planet—was assured him, and a new beginning, with his cash reserves, would be good for him.

James Tyler was good at what he did. The best, he'd have claimed; and from the half-smile on his face, one could not tell whether he spoke in jest. As had Gray, he began by visiting the drug bars in the filthier sections of the City-South. He, too, had been immunized, and the rank smells, the darkness, the almost tangible scent of hatred had no effect upon him.

He sauntered into one dive and sat across from four heavy thugs, the room's only patrons, challenging them to fight merely by offering them a hearty stare and sneer. The first man, an unemployed pavement worker, rose to the challenge in such a bored, mechanical fashion that it almost unsettled Tyler. But Tyler started by crushing the man's foot, then disabled him with horrible thoroughness. The three others fumbled into a charge, one of them groping for a blade. This time Tyler fought dirty, using tricks these simpletons had never dreamed of and were too drug confused to appreciate.

The revenge play came exactly when he expected it. The lights went out, except one ceiling spot that flashed on to reveal him, a perfect target for the battered trio's guns. He already had his sidearm drawn, however, and put the first shot into the light. Next he shot at the bartender who'd switched the lights.

Scattered shots answered him, but he was not where he'd been when he'd first shot. The brief, confused firefight was one of standard slugthrowers, with none of the more expensive laser weapons. Tyler's pistol, however, had a flash-suppressor; when he saw a muzzle flash, he answered it. It took some time before the survivors realized what their quarry was doing.

By the time they switched to knives and began to advance methodically through the darkness, Tyler had slid through the bar to the bartender's lighting panel. Grinning in the dark, he slid a hand across every button available.

In the sudden glare of the room lights and the five remaining spotlights, the thugs froze, only slowly turning toward the bar where their enemy watched them with leveled pistol. There were but two of them, plus the bartender.

Running his fingers through his blond hair, smiling mockingly, he wordlessly invited them to be seated. They declined. One of them considered tossing his blade and wisely decided against it.

"Hello, my friends," Tyler bowed. "There is something I want to know. Maybe you can tell me." He was answered with glooming silence. "All I want to know is . . ." Here he paused and let his smile fade. "Where is Athalos Steldan?"

"I don't know who you mean," answered one; plainly he spoke the truth. It was equally plain that he wished he did know, so as to more fully enjoy rebuffing Tyler.

"Maybe this will help." Tyler, his expression now deadly serious, tossed down a photograph. No one moved to retrieve it. "Pick it up, one of you." His voice was unforgiving; his gun was aimed at the first man's midsection.

"Pick it up," the thick man drawled hatefully, and the bartender gingerly knelt to obey. He looked at it uninterestedly. Tyler, watching him carefully, saw no hint of recognition in the henchman's face. The photograph was passed to the other two; each gave it a perfunctory glance and maintained his poker face. The thick leader flipped it back to the floor. Through the striated drug fumes Tyler saw his face, and there was no expression upon it.

"It's the man they'll give twenty-five grand for. So?"

"Where is he?"

The leader looked at Tyler incredulously. "If I knew that . . ." He said no more.

Tyler reached under the bar and found a heavy wooden club, slender and solid. He tossed it toward the bartender. "Club your friends. Knock them flat. Now." The man stared at Tyler as at a madman. "It's either that, or I start shooting. Him first."

The bartender looked at the third man, and back to Tyler.

"Now."

There was no mistaking the chill in Tyler's eyes. The bartender reached for the club, hefted it, and hovered in indecision.

"Do it," the leader said in a tired voice.

"Wait a minute," the other man yowled. "Boss, wait a minute!"

"Do you want to live?" the leader said without looking at him.

The fellow stopped protesting.

"I want to hear the *clunk*," Tyler said happily, his

grin returning. The fellow stepped forward; Tyler froze him with a quick movement of his gun.

The bartender stepped behind the man, who closed his eyes and tensed. The club came down, hard enough to satisfy Tyler. With a rustle of clothing, the victim crumpled. The bartender had had time to realize that if he was asked to repeat the clubbing, the double shock would be far more dangerous than a single, solid crack.

The bartender refused to step behind his leader, whom he dared not bludgeon. "You club him, instead," Tyler said to the leader. The heavy man, used to giving orders and not to obeying, closed his eyes for a moment to calm his rage, then grabbed the club and slammed it across the bartender's forehead. The smaller man fell soundlessly.

"Nice shot, fatso," Tyler said, showing no emotion. "I think you killed him."

"Saves my partner the job."

"Come along, old friend. Let's go."

"Where to?"

"What do you care?"

The leader said nothing, and followed Tyler's gesture toward the rear of the bar.

"You recognize theatrics when you see them," Tyler observed. "Good. I like my tools sharp." He smiled once more, flashing the leader his intolerable grin. "But not too sharp. Understood?"

Raw hatred was something he knew how to deal with.

Steldan heard of the mass arrest while listening to a radio program with Linde that evening. She had grown little by little more used to him. They still maintained their truce, although the more easy it grew for Linde, the more tense it became for Steldan.

The announcement faded, and music resumed. Linde had paid little attention—weren't arrests behind her now?—although she sensed from Steldan's rapt expression that it was important to him.

"Did you hear?" he asked, abstractedly.

"Arrests of counterfeiters along the Spina in the City-South. I don't see . . ."

But Steldan's mind was elsewhere. He hastily reviewed his operations of the past weeks. Nothing he'd done, he judged, should have had that effect. It should have been an investment, something to take advantage of later. He'd planned, cold-heartedly, on a gang war to run interference for his eventual move. Now he had to act.

Perhaps I should have foreseen this. Perhaps it was the only thing that Danliffe could have done. Part of him was thankful; at least this way fewer people would die.

On the other hand, about half a million are going to be held for ransom, the price of my freedom. If I'm not let go. . . He refused to pursue that thought; with no further regrets, he phoned the satellite relay, and transmitted one word to the gigantic refinery orbiting above the giant planet that provided the fuel to the world of Chirkun.

"Interrogate."

The next day, at noon, a 40,000-ton tanker would land at the Spaceport. It would not arrive unheralded.

Linde, watching him, laid a hand upon his forearm. He grinned at her, a lopsided, unhappy grin. Action was called for, and he didn't have the time for her.

He spent the rest of the night on the telephone, while Linde hovered in the background. At about two-thirty in the morning, he stood, stretched, and noticed her.

"Is something wrong, Linde?" he asked, noting her pale face.

"Tomorrow's the day, isn't it? The day you start your escape?"

Steldan became concerned. "That can't frighten you, can it?"

She shook her head, denying the dismay that her face displayed. "It's not that. It's just . . ."

Steldan looked at her, seeing her expressions, like masks, one, over the other, over. . . His training cut in; his own face became an unreadable, if pleasantly attentive, poker face. And he read her mind as well.

She loves me. I'd suspected much, but not as much as this. She loves me, and dares to hope that I'll come to love her. And I cannot!

And deeper, deeper in his mind, the part of him that

was always alone wondered: *Why not?* What had the Navy ever done to him or for him that demanded his response? Couldn't he leave the universe to itself? Didn't he deserve some happiness?

A life, he with Linde, she with him, painted itself before his imagination. And, although nothing of this showed in his expression, he discovered that he desired her. He wondered for a moment if this was what love felt like.

What the hell can I say?

He wanted to take her in his arms; he wanted . . . He stood, immobile, and willfully hardened his heart. No words would serve. He saw the warmth in Linde's eyes, and he steeled himself to reject it.

Looking at her with compassion that he would not let show, he said merely, "Go to bed, Linde. Get some sleep. Tomorrow will be important."

She wavered, unable for a moment to speak or act. Steldan carefully looked the slightest bit away, neither watching her turmoil nor turning away from her need. She shuddered imperceptibly. Reluctantly, she walked past him toward her bedroom. At the doorway she turned, opened her mouth, closed it.

"Good night," Steldan said to her, very seriously. "Dream not." He looked fully into her eyes for a short time.

Is this what villainy feels like? To balance rejection with caution, to walk the razor's edge . . .

Linde forced a faint smile, and went into her bedroom. Through the thin walls, Steldan could hear her undress, and knew that she didn't weep. Would it have been better if she had? He couldn't guess.

He lay awake on the sofa for an hour, thinking in the darkness. He thought of his plans, and of the long train of events that had brought him here. And, over and over, he thought of Linde.

In the morning, he knew that his dreams had been significant, but he could remember none of them.

Part III
Day of Burning

It was the one hundred and forty-fifth day of the year. It began shaping into a fine, clear day, with not a cloud above. Gentle breezes wafted up the city's canyons, cooling the towering business and residential blocks; even the City-South enjoyed the perfect weather.

Wilth lounged in his maximum-security prison cell and waited for an opportunity to escape. At six o'clock yesterday afternoon, the squadron of C.I.B. enforcers and local policemen had blown in the doors of his counterfeiting shop, capturing fifteen of his engravers. Three others had tried to fight, drawing handguns. Wilth felt no pity for anyone that stupid. One of his men had been more clever; he'd reversed the press, destroying the original plates and leaving their captors with less evidence than they might have taken. It wouldn't matter, though. They had far more evidence than they'd need.

Who had turned him in? That Steldan character didn't know the location of the shop, and he'd had his new engraver, "Douglas," carefully watched. One of his other men? They were too well paid, and his shop seemed free from police pressure. But Danliffe and his organization had been feeling the pressure lately, in a big way.

Wilth swore, and paced agitatedly within his small confinement. One of Danliffe's thugs could have turned him in, in response to imagined past wrongs. Wilth knew, though, that he'd find the man, sooner or later. The traitor would pay. And as for Danliffe . . . Danliffe was as good as arrested, this very moment.

It seemed just likely enough that Danliffe had done this.

At eight, the cold-faced C.I.B. interrogator let himself into the room and without so much as pausing, slammed a hypodermic spray against Wilth's forearm. The small dose of verificants soon slid through the thin man's bloodstream and into his midbrain. He had barely time to feel anger before his consciousness released control of his memory. In a room suddenly tinged a wan yellow, Wilth gave strangely animated answers, revealing anything asked of him, no longer even wondering why.

"Did you cause the Block 10 explosion?"

"For heaven's sake, no."

The C.I.B. man frowned; Wilth saw this and could not care.

"Do you know who did?"

"Hm? No. I thought it was all an accident . . ."

"Have you planned another one?"

"No."

"But you profited from the last one?"

"Yes."

"How?"

"We looted the government files building."

"What did you take?"

"Identification forms and card blanks; central file spools; imprinters; verification fiber blanks."

"And then?"

"We set fire to the place."

The C.I.B. man frowned again. The loss of the government central files had thrown the city, and indeed the entire world, into near chaos. With the blanks, Wilth and his cronies had covered a circle of impersonators, infiltrators, fugitives, and felons of all descriptions. With application, they might have taken over the planet.

"No more questions."

"That's good; I've got lots more secrets." Wilth lay back on his bed-shelf and gazed placidly at the ceiling. The C.I.B. man grinned nastily at the thought of Wilth coming out of the drugged state and remembering the conversation. Although the evidence gained by the chemical interview was of limited use in court, it was invaluable in tracking down other criminals. Wilth would be convicted on other grounds, using the legitimately gained evidence acquired in the raid. And the drugging procedure was repeatable as many times as the C.I.B. wished, to learn from Wilth the exact names and aliases used by the undercover criminals.

At eight-fifteen, after reporting to the coordinator and passing to him the tape of the interview, the C.I.B. interviewer returned to Wilth's cell and gave him another dose of the same drug. Wilth had regained just enough of his self-possession to object, although not enough to struggle.

"There is a freighter loaded with 40,000 tons of fuel from one of the refineries. It belongs to Metroyan's System Freight, the same company that owned the Block 10. Did you know that?"

"Of course not."

"It is scheduled to land and discharge its cargo at noon. Did you know that?"

"How could I have? No."

"There have been formal complaints lodged against its landing, by several protest organizations, including Survivors of Block 10, and the Combined Insurance Companies' Council on Spaceflight. Did you know that?"

"How—No."

"Unofficial complaints are being lodged at the Portmaster's Office; frightened people are leaving the city; court orders prohibiting the landing are being sought. Did you know any of this?"

"No."

Well, the interviewer thought, *somebody has done a grand job of whipping up a mass panic. The Leonidas High Court refuses to grant the landing injuncton, and the Chirkun High Court can't put together a quorum. If an injunction were granted, it would ruin Metroyan's; if it isn't, the panic will do more harm, and Metroyan's will still be ruined.*

And an explosion will kill half a million people.

The morning was yet young, and things were already happening too fast.

"I don't understand. This is the day you plan to escape, and all you've done is make phone calls."

Steldan accepted the soft drink that Linde handed him, and tried to phrase a reply. "You know how powerful the phone is as a tool, a weapon. I'm trying to . . . punch a corridor through the trawl-net wide enough to run through."

"Run to where?"

"Off-planet. That's the most important part. Chirkun is too hot right now."

"I'll want to come with you."

Steldan had expected that, and for some reason it didn't bother him. "You'll have half an hour to pack." She nodded, leaving the room to pick up her necessities. Steldan gazed around the room, seeing the dozens of personal touches, items that were almost a part of Linde's soul. How would she take their loss? In minutes she was back, a small traveling-kit under her arm. Businesslike, she looked at the room, searching for items of importance. She appeared not to even see the collectables, the hourglasses, the artworks.

"We can pull our funds from the banks easily, I suppose?" she said quietly.

"I've taken care of that. By phone. Drafts will be waiting for us at the Spaceport."

Linde half-smiled at the idea. Steldan watched her, seeing her cut herself off from her past without any signs of remorse. She seemed to see *him* as her new life, which bothered him a great deal.

"I like to think of it as a standard planetary assault, in reverse." He spoke, he realized, as much to calm himself as Linde. "When a fleet hits a planet—"

"Like Secretary Telford at Tenh Sonallae?"

Steldan almost gasped. "Um . . . Yeah. He had to clear a corridor through the orbiting fortresses, and through the atmospheric defenses. He couldn't strip the whole sky of foes, just one thin tunnel."

"Then he landed his assault transports through the tunnel." Linde nodded. She'd seen a presentation on popular television documenting the process.

"And from that point, it's out of his hands."

"How much money have you got left?"

"A fair amount. You realize that we'll have to steal a ship?"

"I hadn't thought about it." She seemed happy, as if action, no matter how desperate, was better than the long wait.

"I can't pilot a spaceship," Steldan admitted bluntly.

Linde looked at him quizzically, saying nothing.

"I have a scheme; I have all along. As to whether or not it's crazy . . ."

"I don't know piloting either," Linde said, knowing full well the idiocy of trying to pilot and navigate a spaceship untrained. "Highjacking?"

"Much too dangerous. The safeguards on most ships are virtually unbeatable."

"Not during takeoff, when the computer is busy with control problems."

Steldan said nothing, but deep within him, he rejoiced. Linde was beginning to question him, to see that he was not an ideal leader. If his crackbrained stunt didn't kill both of them, she might even someday see him for what he really was. And, like as not, she'd leave him then. He wasn't, he couldn't be, the sort of man that she wanted to follow.

He hadn't asked for her damned devotion anyway.

"It's even easier than that," he said carefully. "I'll hold the city to ransom, from the ship that will be landing at noon. I'll threaten to blow it up."

"They'd call your bluff."

Would they? He didn't believe it. Softly, facing Linde, he murmured, "What makes you think I'd be bluffing?"

And that did it. As quickly as Linde had tied herself to him, and as totally, she cut herself loose. Her eyes widened; she stared at Steldan more intensely than she'd ever stared at anything before. She *saw* him. He was not her better half; he was not the man with whom she intended to spend the rest of her life; he was not. Every detail of him came sharply to her vision. His behavior: proper, if distant, it seemed then to her. His moral structure: ambiguous. Would he kill thousands of people to free himself? Would he subject the city to another slaughter?

For a moment she wavered. Blind trust was comforting, in its way, and living with one's eyes closed feels safe. The feelings she now experienced *hurt*, in ways she didn't understand. She could go with him. Why not?

"Count me out." The words seemed to come from beyond her, surprising her. Steldan merely nodded.

"Then you won't mind if I bind you, and leave you here?" His face didn't change, and he remained seated.

Again she saw him. His eyes, not in pain, never mocking. What did he feel? A hundred contradictory impulses flashed through her: to run, to fight, to call for help. His eyes, that once she thought she loved.

A final time Steldan nodded; then rose and bound the unresisting woman securely. The cord was soft, and he tied it gently.

Despite his many years' training in psychology, theoretical and practical, Steldan comprehended the enormity of Linde's thoughts only with difficulty. She thought, in her betrayed innocence, that Steldan's crime was planning murder. The truth was even more horrible. Even killing some people is more fair to them than making a tool of them.

It hadn't been my intention, he thought, tightening the knots. *I never planned this.* Her hands were bound apart, wrapped, trapped. *She deserves better.*

She'd had a long moment of freedom, and she'd not shied away from it. Through his remorse—sincere remorse, ironically—Steldan knew that she would some day be free.

"I must go," he said, low and shamefacedly. Gently, so carefully gently, he lifted her and set her into a closet, shutting the door upon the first person he'd ever dared to love.

The Captain of the Freighter *Goldfisch* was unaware of the turmoil below. The titanic hull moved in a skewing approach toward the planet, so that if its engines failed it would merely swing past and be lost in emptiness. It was a nice idea, he supposed, but ridiculous. To land on something, you eventually had to aim for it; there was no avoiding the final danger of a hard set-down. The *Goldfisch* had once been named the *Block 14,* and had been hastily renamed after the death of the *Block 10.*

Landing approach policy was as strained and overcautious as mathematics could make it; computers backed up computers, which backed up more computers. *Goldfisch*'s engines, redesigned, could throw her out of close orbit with ease. Her hull was four times as thick as it had any need to be.

And people were frightened. And rightfully.

"Bah!" the Captain grumbled, overwatching his navigation mate at the controls. He had no patience with safety precautions. For the thousandth time he glared at the destruct triggers built into the control room. Should it look like the ship was about to crash, the triggers would be tripped, either from here or by radio control from the Spaceport. "And how many people would die from the impact of 40,000 tons of burning fuel?" he asked of no one in particular. His control room crew ignored him, by now used to his perpetual state of outrage. What he needed was a good, loud fight with the portmaster.

It was now eight-thirty; in three hours he'd have to hand over control of his ship to the landing-grid computers, which would land his ship more accurately and safely than he himself could.

"Bah!" he growled again. For him, piloting had long since lost all its charm.

Tyler's capture of his man in the bar had been a cursed slow way of getting information. Tyler admitted as much to himself; over the hours, he slowly worked over his prisoner. In time, he dragged forth more information than the man had known that he'd known.

Tyler's interrogation style was brutal, unlovely, and reasonably effective. Lacking the training to do a systematic job, he simply ripped the information from the man by mild torture. Neither that procedure, nor the more violent one of severe torture, would have cracked a trained prisoner. The thug, however, was merely one of Danliffe's band of small-time racketeers.

Moaning over what were actually no more than wide bruises, he whined to Tyler over and over: "I don't know. I don't—"

Tyler silenced him with a tired nudge. *Could it actually be that this idiot doesn't know anything useful at all? Ridiculous!* He decided that he needed a new approach.

"Let's go over what you've already told me," he said levelly. "When things fail to mesh, I'll know you're lying." Tyler knew damned well that the fellow wasn't lying; he merely wanted to find Steldan. In this, the essential difference between Tyler and Gray showed up. Gray was capable of using a varied approach, following several leads at once. Tyler thought in intensities, extremes. While he was capable of subtlety, he preferred to act directly, and to follow one trail to the finish.

For the past few hours it had not paid off; that was about to change.

Rambling, in an incoherent fashion, the thug once again spoke of the many bounty hunters combing the city for Steldan. This time, however, he mentioned one who had dropped from the chase. She had been tall, dark-haired, lovely. . . . Tyler slapped him, trying to get him to stay on one subject. The criminal, taking it as an order to be more specific, dragged her name from his memory: "Linde Volke."

"So?"

"I just thought . . ."

"Don't. When did she disappear?"

"She didn't disappear; she just quit. Went home and . . ."

"And what?"

"She gave up the chase for Steldan. I don't know why."

"When?"

"A week and a few days ago."

Tyler decided that the man was no longer of use to him. He tied the exhausted criminal securely and rolled him under a table in the abandoned apartment flat he'd been using for a torture chamber.

"Linde Volke, eh?"

"Yes."

"What is her address?"

A last flash of lucidity returned to the abused man. "Look it up in the phone book, bastard."

Tyler raised an eyebrow at this man who so eagerly wanted to die. His hand caressed his gun butt.

Ah, well, he relented. *I'll save my appetite.*

In twenty minutes he arrived at Linde's flat, surprisingly near in the complicated warren that was the CitySouth's interior. He had the lock open in minutes. No one seemed to be present, and yet. . . .

He stalked to a closet, and flung it open. Inside, on the floor, Linde lay, bound tightly, her wide eyes gratefully resting upon her rescuer. Tyler bent down and removed her gag.

"You've got to stop him!" she said intently. "He's mad!"

"Athalos Steldan?"

"Yes. He's heading for the Spaceport."

"I'll find him, and stop him before he hurts anyone. Don't worry." He winked in a friendly fashion—and reaffixed the gag, before Linde had time to protest. "Bye, now," he said cheerily, and shut the closet door, closing off his view of her wide and tearful eyes.

Ron Gray, in his persona as the engraver Douglas, had not been at Wilth's print shop when the C.I.B. raided it. The first he knew of it was when a squad of C.I.B. riot police kicked in his hotel room door and hit him from three angles with stun-beams. His limp form was hauled away by three of the C.I.B. medics attached to the squad. He awoke in prison, at 9:18.

"Hello," a medic greeted him. "Can you hear me?"

"Um . . . yeah," Gray answered, opening and closing his eyes several times to relieve their feeling of grainy numbness.

"Any pain?"

"No."

"You're sure?"

"Yeah. Why—?"

The medic, by way of response, slammed the hypodermic against Gray's arm. The verificants in Gray's bloodstream had been chemically altered by the Navy. In it, the verificants dissipated with a small release of heat. The warm sensation under his skin informed him of the nature of the dose: truth drugs, and the dosage size: moderate.

When he failed to fall into the relaxed state, the medic showed his first surprise. "How . . . ?" he stammered. Swiftly he rose and triggered an alarm. Gray sat, smiling at him.

In moments, a troop of prison guards arrived, sliding the cell door open and entering in pairs. The guard-Captain, a small, agile man in black and red, entered last, took in the situation, and motioned his troops to wait outside.

"He's been immunized to the truth drug," the medic said needlessly. "I thought that might mean he was dangerous."

The guard-Captain ignored him, and deactivated the alarms. "An interviewer will be here shortly. We'll wait."

Gray sat through it all, awake, conscious, and plainly amused. He had no intention whatever of trying to explain to these men who were but lower-grade deputies. His story could wait for someone with some authority.

Not long afterward, an officer with that authority arrived. The medic and the guard-Captain told their stories, and finally Gray was allowed to tell his.

After virtually an hour of checking, double-checking, and administrative running around, Gray was released. He parted with the flustered prison commissioner, and caught a train for the Spaceport.

Only when he arrived back at his offices did anyone bother to tell him the day's details.

"Forty thousand tons? And we're at ground zero?"

"Yessir." Harcourt, seeing her superior unaware of the facts, had wasted no time filling him in. Gray listened, fascinated.

"I thought it was *you* who had caught me," he said when she had finished, referring to his feigned flight and her attempts to have him pursued.

"Nope. Half the crooks in this city are in prisons right now. A third of them are going to be sent to off-planet prisons for life, on charges of murder."

"Who turned them in?"

"Well, that's not my province, but I have heard some neat rumors. It was an anonymous phone call—"

"Steldan?"

"Definitely not. I've checked that far. It was probably someone higher up in the underworld hierarchy." She watched Gray, who seemed at a loss for a course of action. For once, she stood in the doorway, not peering over the room divider, probably because her computer presently worked unsupervised on a very large, low-level search. "Before the call came in, revealing the location of the forgery base, other phone calls had been coming in, giving away criminal leaders."

Gray's gaze wandered up from his desk top toward Harcourt. "You hadn't mentioned that yet."

"Well, here's how it seems to me. I think that Steldan had been informing on criminals in one branch of the illegal organization, and making it look like members of some other branch had done it. The calls were scattered about the city, probably through the use of a false-coder—"

Gray snapped into alertness. "What kind of false-coder?"

"How many kinds are there?"

Gray didn't answer. After a moment of thought, he arrived at a decision. "You and your planetary C.I.B. have helped me a great deal. I'll return part of the favor. Using my Navy authorization, look into the Restricted Technology File." He gave her a string of reference numbers.

Harcourt walked around the partition into her half of the room, and worked for a moment at her computer. Her voice drifted back to Gray. "O.K., then. What is it?"

"You should have a circuit diagram on your screen?"

"Um . . . yeah."

"It's a device to bypass the signals sent by false-coders. And if your C.I.B. recorded those phone calls—"

"They did."

"—We can trace the calls *now*, after they've been made, and after the caller thinks he's safe."

Harcourt said nothing, keying in the instructions to transmit the diagram and information to the C.I.B. lab elsewhere in the city. Tagging it with a "top priority" flag, she ensured that it would be seen and no doubt appreciated as soon as possible.

"Now we wait?" she asked.

"With that tanker—*Goldfisch*, wasn't it?—on its way down?" He thought carefully. "I don't have the authority to stop it. I'm not sure I'd want to stop it. It would set a bad precedent . . ."

"Would Commander Tyler have that authority?"

"Tyler." Gray spoke the name uncertainly. Why had his superiors at Sector Headquarters decided to replace him? It made no sense. Certainly it had been a long hunt, with concrete results lacking, but that was common during this kind of operation.

It was now 10:35. If all hell were to break loose in an hour and a half, he wanted to know where he stood.

"Can we contact Tyler? I understand that he dug in, the same way I did. Going undercover . . ."

"He did," Harcourt answered, and stuck her head over the room divider. The antic reassured Gray; it was a point of friendly madness in a city currently ruled by malefic insanity. "He left his aide, a humorless little stinker named Rolle, in charge here. I haven't seen him all day, and I haven't bothered to call him."

"Why not?"

"All he ever says is: 'Carry on, as you were.'"

"But you said he outranks me?"

"Well, Tyler said he has seniority . . ."

"Call him. He may need to take charge." *I could be accused of passing the buck, of hiding behind a superior when the difficult or dangerous decisions come up.* That, though, was better than making a wrong decision, and being held responsible for that as well as for usurping command. If Rolle were dangerous, he finally decided, he could relieve him on some technicality.

The next half hour, Gray spent on the phone, feeling his way back into the situation. Twenty minutes into the phoning, Rolle arrived, flatly deferred command to Gray, and sat in a corner reading magazines. Gray stared at the tidy little man, not knowing whether to feel relief or annoyance.

He was soon in contact with the assembled Chirkun Supreme Judiciary, meeting now in an armored chamber somewhere beneath the new Leonidas Government Office Building. In a few sentences he apprised them of the situation with respect to his quarry, Steldan. The Justices muttered among themselves, considering this in light of the information already available to them.

"Could he detonate the ship?" asked one.

"I honestly don't know," Gray answered. He wished for a visual link in place of the voice-only conference circuit he was now part of.

"By beaming a destruct frequency at the ship,"

Harcourt whispered in Gray's ear. Gray, trying to listen to her and to two Justices arguing, shook his head.

"Frequency's secret," he muttered back. "And it's been changed. . . . Check on that, will you?" Harcourt rushed back to her half of the room. Her computer easily verified the change, effective seventeen minutes ago. The change was pseudorandomized; she knew from the brief description of the method that she'd be unable to predict the current frequency.

She wrote: "Freq. changed at 10:56. That's safe," on a corner of paper. Back in Gray's part of the office, she put it in his hand. He read it, and nodded.

"I think that the landing is safe. We can't come up with anything else . . ." He looked up at Harcourt, who seemed doubtful.

"I refuse to take chances," a Justice snarled in the background.

"We seem to be split six-five," another said softly.

"Which way does the opinion lean?" Gray asked, a sick feeling of helplessness upon him. This court, exactly like the Court of the Supreme Judiciary upon Archive, needed at least a two-vote difference before an "opinion" became a "decision." Like all other pretenses toward checks and balances, it merely served to strengthen the power of the Praesidium.

"Well, it's not a formal vote . . ." the Justice said pedantically, "but we seem to be in favor of 'no action.' We'll let you know if that changes. For now, bring that ship down. Safely."

Their rules were a crippling idiocy. At least, in the Supreme Judiciary at Archive, Justicar Solme had his Praesidium vote; here, each Justice was equal. Gray let his mind wander, envisioning the men of the Praesidium. *They* had no such two-vote-margin rule to slow them down; a four-three vote had the force of law. Did that explain why each member was so like a feudal lord in his own domain?

Steldan was Gray's domain, and he'd damned well bring him in. Another quick check with Harcourt showed him that Steldan had never actually threatened to explode that ship. Indeed, Steldan couldn't be linked at all, so far.

The ship would land in forty-two minutes. Was that actually the deadline? No. In thirty-six minutes, or six minutes before noon, the *Goldfisch* would be close enough to ruin the city if it should blow. Thirty-six minutes in which to be certain that Steldan was disarmed.

"Harcourt," Gray called.

"Yessir?"

"What about that phone-tracing system I gave you? Have your people got it working yet?"

"Um . . . Just a second, while I inquire . . ." Gray worked his own computer controls to look into the abbreviated reports of the calls fingering the criminals.

"They've got it working perfectly, and they have an address."

"Which set of calls?"

"The earlier ones. The later set is only one call, and they have an address for it, too."

"Well, send squads to raid them, dammit!"

Harcourt let the outburst hover for a moment before answering. "They've thought of that. They expect simultaneous break-ins in a very few minutes."

"Why haven't I been kept up to date?"

She put her head over the room divider and scrutinized Gray. "I think it's because they care more about half a million casualties than about your fugitive." Gray glared at her. She was right, of course, but Steldan was very likely the key to the whole situation.

Five minutes had passed when the word came that two people had been captured. The first was a fat criminal named Danliffe, who would have escaped unnoticed, except for the alarm his I.D. card had triggered when he showed it. The second was a woman named Linde Volke, who had been tied in a closet.

Steldan was unaccounted for.

The Tanker *Goldfisch* surrendered control to the Spaceport Navigation computers, which eased it into the invisible funnel of gravitic forces generated by the landing grid. The captain had been informed of the problems below, and his fury increased to a towering rage. After a quick radio call to his superiors at Metroyan's System Freight, he knew that he either landed and unloaded the fuel, or he single-handedly ruined the company.

The shipboard computers, backing up the Spaceport's larger ones, assured him that all was normal. Banks of green lights, signaling the status of everything from engine pressure to radio down-link, promised a safe landing. There was even a green light that claimed none of the other green lights was wrongly illuminated.

In less than twenty minutes, the controllers at the Spaceport would have him set down; two hours after that, all his fuel would be pumped out into gigantic holding tanks. Three days later, his ship, scrubbed, fine-tuned, and refueled, would be on its way back to the cluster of orbiting refineries about the titan gas-planet Beta.

I won't be aboard, though, he thought angrily. Pilots, navigators, and Captains were rotated. He'd earned a five-week vacation. And a hell of a lot of pay. Combat pay. He never knew whether to laugh or cry at that; he got combat pay, while the planetary airspace defense command pilots on routine patrol did not.

Speaking of which . . . He grabbed the radio microphone again and signaled the Spaceport. A tense traffic controller asked his business.

"What are those two Scouts doing up here, anyway?"

"I don't know. Why?"

"Were they there to blast me if I started to fall?"

"I don't think so. They've been orbiting up there for weeks now. It's Navy business."

"Well, they gave me a hell of a looking-over."

"One of them paralleled your course for a few minutes. Big deal. Do you need anything else?"

"Goldfisch out." Things were happening, faster than the captain liked. Fifteen minutes now: the tensest part. It was now irreversible, should the grid-field fail. His ship would be detonated immediately, the fuel bursting in an expanding blot that would ignite explosively as it hit the atmosphere.

Or, should the field fail in the last five minutes or so, a twelve-kilometer fireball would scorch the city, killing hundreds of thousands of people.

* * *

"And you must be Athalos Steldan."

Steldan froze, shivering. The bright sunlight took on a yellow tinge; the sunlit streets, crowded now with the late-morning pedestrian traffic, swam for a moment in his vision.

Not having been shot yet, he turned, unsteadily, to face his captor. Tyler stood before him, grinning, his blond hair stirred by the cool breeze. In his gray eyes was an alertness, an animation rare for him. He held his well-worn pistol tight in his right hand.

"Let's get inside, shall we? Before we attract unwanted attention. I'm Commander James Tyler; I'll be your assassin."

"A smiling killer. I'm honored." And because he had no choice, he moved in the direction that Tyler indicated. In this part of the City-South, no one would dream of intervening in a capture of this type. Steldan could have shouted or leaped, and it would simply have gotten him killed sooner.

They passed through the doorway of an empty drug bar, stooping to clear the low lintel. Through the murky interior they strolled, Tyler covering Steldan.

"Here," Tyler said. "Against that wall. That should do nicely."

"Just like that?" Steldan asked.

"Just like this." The gun spat twice, the heavy bullets missing the frantically rolling Steldan and embedding themselves in the wall. Tyler smiled at Steldan's desperately clumsy dash for cover, and abstained from killing him . . . yet.

From a hastily gained covert behind an overturned table, Steldan called: "I'm armed!"

Tyler stood in the open, unconcerned. He always enjoyed resourceful victims. "No, you're not." There was no exit from the trap; both doors, front and back, were easily within his field of fire. He put two shots into the thick table top, just for amusement.

Tyler stood relaxed, ready. Steldan would probably make his move soon; he'd throw something heavy, for a distraction, to cover a dash for the door.

Instead, Steldan began to roll the table along on its

edge, keeping squarely behind it while he crept toward the back door.

Nice try, thought Tyler. *But nothing keeps me from taking that table away from him, and blowing his head open. And there! His foot is sticking out, unprotected.* Shooting a victim in the foot never had satisfied Tyler; it shortened the struggle too much.

Ah, now he throws something. Tyler effortlessly dodged the hurled object—a grimy, lidless jar—and grinned happily when the rolling table came to a passage too narrow to be negotiated. Steldan was stuck between the bar itself and some other inverted tables. There was no way to clear the obstacles without exposing himself to fire.

And now the hunt began to bore Tyler; a sick sense of ennui filled him. Soon it must end, with a bleeding corpse lying inert upon the floor. At that, the inner Tyler, the man within the man, would again go to sleep, to be roused only dimly by wisecracks, practical jokes, and brutality. He felt almost physically sleepy. Murder is so little to sustain oneself upon.

"Come out, Steldan, and die." The grin was gone. The blond hair seemed gray in the room's half-light. And the vibrancy had left the cold, gray, killer's eyes, leaving only a bottomless well of loneliness. "Come out, and be blown apart."

A stirring, a rush, and Steldan heaved the table at his tormentor. Tyler easily sidestepped, alertness returning, while Steldan leaped over and behind the bar.

Now it was Tyler's turn to scramble, and he did so with reckless haste. Drug dens have weapons behind the bar, pistols or shotguns. The danger brought him fully back to awareness, and he acutely enjoyed the sensation. The hunt was *fun* again, and a challenge once more.

Steldan did indeed find a good assortment of weapons, in a cabinet built into the back of the bar. There were three good clubs, short, thick, and perfectly balanced, two pistols, and a short-barreled shotgun. He knew how to use the firearms, but not with the proficiency that Tyler had displayed. In a heavy exchange of fire, Steldan must lose.

How does one determine where his enemy is when

neither man dares raise his head? For Steldan it was worse. Tyler probably had his eyes above the level of his covert, his gun already leveled.

"Come out, Steldan," mocked Tyler. "Make it easy on yourself." The only reply he received was the unmistakable sound of a shell being levered into the chamber of the shotgun. In a few minutes, he knew, Steldan would thrust his head above the bar, for a look-see. Would he peer at the right end, the left end, or the middle? *It's like a pop-up target at the firing range.* To the far left of Tyler's field of fire, where the bar ended, a shadowed spot caught his eye. *Will Steldan stick his head out at the bar's end, flat to the floor? It's pretty obvious . . .* He aimed his pistol at that spot, ready for the slightest hint of movement.

He saw what he was waiting for, and let fly. Even as his two bullets shattered the plastic box that Steldan had thrust out, Tyler saw Steldan's head appear over the bar, two meters from the left end.

"No fair," Tyler laughed. "You're thinking!"

"You, friend, are insane," Steldan answered. He'd found, in another cabinet, the possible answer to his problems: the bar's main circuit breaker. And yet. . . . . The thought of a fight in the darkness frightened him more, even, than Tyler did already. He sat, gripping the shotgun, and tried to compose himself.

Tyler put two shots into the front of the bar, where he guessed Steldan to be, then replaced the clip. He knew full well that his bullets weren't penetrating the thick wood, but it was certain to keep Steldan worried. He had lots of time. He could have used hand grenades—if he'd had them—and no one would have investigated the noise.

Lots of time.

It was the last thing Steldan had to spare. He'd left a recorded message on the phoning false-coder, which would soon automatically transmit it to the city's central police switchboard. He didn't know, however, that the message, coder and all, was in the hands of the planetary C.I.B. Soon they would send a copy to Gray. Soon. Steldan, expecting the message to go out in ten minutes, glanced at his watch. It was now twelve minutes before noon. He was already behind schedule, unaware of how far behind he'd fallen.

Two more bullets slammed into the wood, not piercing it. Steldan threw two bottles in high arcs over the bar, waited for a split-second, then lifted the shotgun over the bar and fired blind. The spray of small pellets fanned out into the room, breaking glass and embedding themselves in exposed wooden surfaces. A double echo jarred through the room as Tyler responded.

Neither was injured.

" 'You can't win, you can't break even, and you can't get out of the game,' " Tyler quoted.

And a tie means we both lose, Steldan finished silently. "A literate assassin," he muttered aloud. "I thought you guys mostly grunted."

"No, we tend to be relatively articulate. It's more fun that way."

Steldan made a hasty decision, and with it, fear came. His heart knocked; he couldn't seem to get a full breath of air. He was about to leap into the open, braving the fire of Tyler's gun; he was about to jump headlong at death. And in his mind, he found that the fear he felt was most reminiscent of stage fright, when one hesitates that last fraction of a second before stepping from the wings.

He did it with one, sweeping motion. His hand swept down, brushing the circuit breakers, plunging the room into gray semidarkness. That downward swing of arm, joined with a great stretch of legs, sent him up on top of the bar, astradde it, face down. Momentum carried him on, down to the floor, where he half rolled, half hurled himself across the killing space.

Tyler had been taken by surprise, expecting more firefight banter. He'd judged Steldan to be too cowardly, too reserved.

It was too late to react. Steldan landed heavily against the tip-tilted table behind which Tyler hid, and his full body block slammed the heavy wood top into Tyler. Steldan recovered first, stood, and knocked aside Tyler's gun barrel even as he stared into it. With strength born of utter desperation, he lifted the massive table a little and crashed it down upon Tyler's ankle.

Not waiting for death, he turned and fled, low and zigzagging, to the door.

He threw himself out, up the stairs, and onto the street. There he scrambled to his knees, then to his feet, and staggered off. He'd more than half expected a bullet between his shoulder blades.

The citizens on the street, seeing a dusty man in dingy clothing gasping for breath and staggering into a run, shied away. When it was plain that he was running for his life, they pulled back, alert for whatever pursued him. There was no interference, and no pursuit.

Steldan brushed himself off, caught his breath, and hurried toward the Spaceport. There was only one way out, and that was forward.

The first deadline passed without incident. The tanker *Goldfisch* was just six minutes from landing, and all was normal. But should the ship explode now . . . Ron Gray forced himself not to think about it.

"Tape for you, sir!" Harcourt called. "It's from Steldan." Gray grabbed up his phone and heard the tape that Steldan had made earlier, being played for him from the C.I.B. station that had found it. He listened with half his attention while Harcourt quietly explained how the tape had been found in the apartment with the bound bounty hunter.

"It is now twelve o'clock," the tape began. *Definitely Steldan*, Gray thought; he'd heard other tapes of the voice of the man he'd never really met. *But it's not twelve o'clock! Not yet!*

"The Tanker from Beta has landed," the voice continued. "If what I ask of you is not granted, immediately, without question, it will explode—"

"Harcourt! Have they done anything about this?" He knew that a ship this close to landing cannot easily be boosted clear. Plainly, however, someone at the C.I.B. headquarters had already heard this tape. Gray was more frustrated than he'd ever felt before.

"Um. A report coming in . . . The ship is being boosted away, using the main grid, plus its own engines . . . at maximum acceleration."

"How long until the city's safe?"

"Takeoff is slower than landing . . . The report says about eleven and a half minutes."

Gray shook his head. He asked his phone to replay the tape from Steldan, so that he could listen more closely.

". . . It will explode, doing what damage you know. If you open your office door, you will find me waiting outside. We had best talk." The tape ended.

Gray sat motionless, amazed at the audacity of anyone who would try such a trick, anyone who would walk into such danger, with the death of a city for a dead man switch. He hesitantly stood and approached the door. Pistol drawn, he stabbed the open button, and leaned out carefully. He gazed up and down the hall. No one was present.

Of course! he exulted. *The message was found early! That means . . .*

It meant that he had a chance, a slim, outside chance. He gave the orders for a trap to be set in the hallway outside.

Soon fifteen men from the Portmaster's office were stationed at the hallway's corners, looking, Gray hoped, like civilians. Each bore stunners, glue-grenades, and other non-lethal weapons. Gray had ordered capture, not killing.

"It is now twelve o'clock," the tape had said; Steldan was known for his punctuality. The remaining minutes passed. Noon arrived. Steldan was nowhere to be seen. In seven minutes, the *Goldfisch* would be beyond the range judged hazardous to the city.

Gray idly watched the flashing lights on his telephone console, displaying the hundreds of phone calls from all over the city, protesting the *Goldfisch*'s landing. The calls were being filtered out, or answered by computers fitted with answering programs. These computers spoke to the callers, said nice things, promised action, and hung up. *Chirkun is due for an overreaction,* Gray judged. A fuel shortage could not be far off. And when the people got fuel-hungry enough, the systemfreight companies would have a revenge, of sorts.

Overreaction, overresponse, and on, and on. On every planet, in each subsector, the massive wheels of government spun, until by their own flywheel mass they turned too far, and only with difficulty were slowed . . . too much. Events worked the same way.

Noon passed.

At six minutes after, Gray joined the troops in the hallway. There was nothing more he could do in his office, and time was still on the wrong side. The last minute passed, and suddenly the *Goldfisch* was beyond the plotted safety radius. Should it explode now, the only people certain to die were the crew. Falling scraps of metal could account for dozens more, but the thousands were safe.

Steldan was nowhere to be seen.

Gray motioned a trooper closer. "Hand me your radio." The trooper, a youngish Marine Sergeant, silently passed the small device to Gray.

Plugging in the earpiece, Gray listened for a while as the advanced observers periodically checked in. In the Spaceport promenade, some pedestrian traffic still tarried, although most people had chosen to leave the scene of the feared disaster.

Fifteen minutes passed heavily. The city was safe now, down to the last citizen. The only people in any danger were aboard the *Goldfisch* . . . and in the hallway with Gray. Would Steldan grab a hostage? Or would he retreat, knowing his plan had failed?

But at this point Athalos Steldan didn't know his plan had failed. A scout in plainclothes, watching from the high balcony overlooking the promenade, spotted a man fitting Steldan's description. The suspect was too far away to be clearly identified against the small photograph all Spaceport personnel carried.

Gray, hearing the report, wondered. The crew of the *Goldfisch* was distinctly expendable; his orders left that point clear. He would bend every effort to keep them safe, but he would not let Steldan go.

The suspect was indeed Steldan. As he rounded the corner, awaiting a trap, he was surprised to see none. The taped message should have been played over twenty-five minutes ago. He walked forward, carrying a small silver box ahead of him. His thumb rested awkwardly over it, suggesting that a switch or button was being held down. Then he stopped. The hallway was silent, which, he realized, could only mean that they were waiting for him.

Gray stepped from a doorway to confront his quarry. Steldan faced him.

"It won't work, Steldan. It won't work."

Steldan returned his gaze, not moving. Gray was unable to guess what passed through his mind.

"You're right," Steldan shrugged at last. "It won't." With that, he flipped the box backward over his shoulder and raised his hands. "I'll surrender instead."

"Just like that?"

"Just like . . . Yeah." He put on a wry face. "Even to keep myself alive, I couldn't doom an entire city. To do it and die anyway is even more pointless."

Gray watched him carefully, alert for any surprises. There were none.

"The tanker was boosted clear, once we got your message. Your ploy was useless."

Steldan, as he was led off, had to agree.

The report soon came to Gray from the bomb detail: the small silver box was a solid chunk of scrap aluminum, entirely harmless.

Two days later a pair of contradictory orders came to Gray on the Courier from Subsector Headquarters. From Grand Admiral Telford, there was an execution order, authorizing Gray to have Steldan killed if caught, or to kill him during capture if he were to resist. The other order was from Deacon Anse, countersigned by Justicar Solme, to bring Steldan alive to Sector Headquarters for questioning, and by no means to take him to a Navy prison.

Steldan had explained much to Gray in those two days, raising questions that could not easily be dispelled. The day before the orders arrived, Steldan had claimed to Gray that he was not the one who'd engineered the disaster at First Binary.

"But you'd say that anyway, guilty or not," Gray objected.

"Telford gave that order, dooming the fleet. I wasn't at the battle, only this long afterward I realized what had happened. I prepared a confidential report and sent it upward through the chain of command, hoping that it would be seen by the proper people. It didn't get far."

"Or," Gray suggested, "you didn't prepare any such report, and are lying to save your skin."

"Then why is Commodore Rudolfs in prison? He wasn't connected with the Battles of Binary in any way."

Gray had no answer for that. Rudolfs, the Chief of Intelligence Records, had been assigned to a totally different sector during the Sonallan crisis. Rudolfs, in prison: that had been the fact that Gray had earlier known and couldn't recall. Did it verify or contradict Steldan's story?

Steldan awaited Gray's decision in a high-security cell in the Leonidas prison, enclosed behind thick walls and the best detection systems on the planet. The room was a cube three meters on a side, with a fold-down bed-shelf, sanitary facility, and two-way viewscreen. Indirectly lighted, air-conditioned, painted a soft mint-green, it was a comfortable place; the warders were quite good about giving him reading material.

In the midafternoon, the viewscreen lit up, and a uniformed warder announced a visitor. Steldan accepted, and the guard's face on the screen was replaced with Linde's.

They looked at each other for a moment, Linde seeing the man she'd admired as strong sitting in confinement and accepting it, while Steldan saw the woman he'd pitied as weak standing proudly through her sorrow.

"Hello, Linde."

"You gave up. You stopped fighting. Why?"

"It couldn't be done. One man can't fight a world."

"And now you sit, and read, and accept. You should fight!"

"How? I've explained what I could to Gray, and when he has time, he'll decide what's to become of me."

"And what about that Tyler maniac?"

"I've talked to Gray about him. He thinks I'm trying to escape, or worse, by spreading dissension."

"Are you?"

Steldan looked at her, unsure as always of what exactly she thought.

"You worship action, dynamism," he charged her.

"That's fine. But the time had come when I could no longer fight."

"Don't even try," sneered Linde, hoping to sting Steldan from his apathy. She was surprised to find the bitterness within her, bitterness that made Steldan's surrender seem like a betrayal.

"I did my best, and failed." He said this as if it explained everything, and suddenly realized that it did not. Linde didn't want him weak.

"Why didn't you turn and run? You could have hidden in the City-South as long as you needed."

"I could have spent the rest of my life hiding, from the Navy, from the criminals, from the police. Always watching, always carving escape routes . . . It wasn't worth it." Linde, it was plain, would not allow herself to understand.

Because he had to, he tried a final time to explain. "Linde, can you understand that I'm unimportant? That all my life, I've been trained to strive for something beyond me? My loyalty has not been diminished by the Navy's treatment of me; my loyalty has been strengthened. My duty is to the Navy, and, more importantly, to the Concordat of Archive."

He smiled, and continued. "I'm also enough of a troublemaker to know that my service to them will always be somewhat individualistic . . . Never mind. I couldn't face a life led only for myself. That wouldn't be meaningless; it would be obscene. I myself will not be the reason for my life."

Linde flared in anger. "Isn't what *you* want the most important thing?"

"No," Steldan said, softly and honestly. "It can't be."

"So, you're just an ant in a hill. One part in a machine."

Do ants have secret police? Do machines have revolutions? He spread his hands. "I have no answer. You asked why I quit, why I didn't turn and run for my life. I walked in there carrying the truth, to be delivered to the Praesidium on my own terms. Now a captive, perhaps they'll hear it on *their* terms. But with me alone in the city, the truth would never have been heard. And, Linde, that message wasn't just mine: it was *me.*"

"That important?"

"That deadly."

Linde's face fell. "You would *not* have been alone! You would have been with me. Damn it, I love you."

What he felt for her likewise rose from his heart and choked him; he was prouder than it, however. He'd spent too much of his life murdering his emotions, crushing the flowering thoughts and sensitivities . . . why? He wanted her; he longed to stay forever by her side.

Gently, he said only: "I dare not love you, Linde. We shall not meet again."

"Don't give up, ever." With that, she turned and left the viewscreen. The warder, face immobile, checked back with Steldan. Satisfied that all was normal, he switched off.

Don't even try, Steldan thought to himself in his isolation. *Oh, well, it's too damned late now.* He knew that if he had it to do over, he would surrender just the same. His false threat to destroy the city had been his best effort.

But if I had it to do over, would I be able to leave Linde?

He wasn't certain he'd ever be able to answer that.

What was to become of him?

James Tyler, when he returned to Gray's office, was unpleasantly surprised by the two orders. It was obvious that Telford was under pressure; for him to openly order Steldan's death was a sign of deep trouble. While the matter had been in Tyler's hands as an unofficial matter, Steldan's demise could have been passed over as merely a convenient accident. In the company of underworld forgers, he would have been written off as another gangland victim. Now it was a matter of record that Telford needed Steldan dead.

Tyler's second surprise was that Gray refused to relinquish command.

"These orders are addressed to me," Gray stated. "I intend to obey the one from the Justicar."

Tyler looked at Gray, his face controlled, his eyes blazing. "I outrank you, Mister."

"And Solme outranks Telford."

"Praesidium members enjoy coequal status."

"The extra vote belonging to Parke devolves onto Solme's office before Telford's."

"You belong to Telford's branch. I can order your arrest."

"Steldan, at present, is in a C.I.B. prison, under the authority of Chirkun, not the Concordat. You can arrest me, but you can't prevent me from making my report. By the time the C.I.B. can be persuaded to release Steldan, further orders from Sector Headquarters will have arrived." Gray paused to pour himself a cup of coffee. He hated the stuff, but felt that a cup of hot chocolate in front of Tyler might be embarrassing. Tyler stood motionless, regarding Gray intensely.

"Is it true," Gray asked softly, "that you accosted Steldan in an empty drug bar?"

Tyler displayed no surprise. "Steldan is a dangerous maniac. He is to be executed at once. You are relieved."

Gray lifted his gaze to the ceiling. "I would be interested in the C.I.B.'s ballistics analysis of the bullets taken from that bar. I don't suppose you'd care to surrender your pistol for a comparison firing? You don't have to; as a Navy officer, you enjoy certain immunities . . .

"Steldan? Executed? I think not. Who can you appeal to? The Portmaster is the Navy's highest ranking officer on the planet, and you won't get far with him." That was the truth; the Portmaster was holding himself as aloof as possible from this fracas. Gray considered petitioning for Tyler's arrest, and decided to save that for a threat if he needed one.

Tyler, for his part, was without recourse. Gray had all the cards. As Telford's assassin, however, Tyler was not helpless; he'd been given coded authorizations to use in emergencies. There were at least two men who would obey him, men who had been sent here by Telford to prevent Steldan's escape.

"You haven't won, Gray. Sooner or later, I'll have your head for this." He spun and left, followed closely by his aide Rolle. They went directly to the Portmaster's office, where Tyler tried to arrange Gray's arrest and removal from command.

The Portmaster, a tired civil servant of a man for all his Navy rank, refused to move against Gray.

"I'm sorry; I truly am." He looked more than sorry; he looked positively embarrassed.

"He is disobeying direct commands from the Secretary," Tyler stated. Why did all these people wish to spare Steldan? "I strongly suggest that he be dealt with."

"But Gray's orders are more specific than yours." He tried to smile. It didn't help. "And Telford's orders were addressed to him . . ." Realizing that he was almost whining, the Portmaster shut himself up.

Tyler, understanding that no action was forthcoming, asked to be loaned a communications booth, to report to his superiors. The Portmaster, anguished at the thought of how that report would reflect upon him, nevertheless agreed. He ushered Tyler and Rolle to a bank of enclosed relay transmitters, privately screened behind sliding panels. Rolle, at a signal from Tyler, made a point of walking with the Portmaster away from the booths, and closing the man outside.

Tyler, knowing that Rolle would guard him vigilantly, stepped within a booth and slid shut the door. Inside the small cubicle were the several radio consoles, for speed-of-light traffic throughout the system. For interstellar communication, he would radio the message to a waiting Courier Ship, which would leave soon to relay the message to its destination.

This wasn't Tyler's intention, although he wanted the Portmaster to think it was. In truth, it was safer for both Tyler and for Telford if the Secretary did *not* know how the illicit mission progressed. And at this point it progressed poorly.

Instead, he tuned the radio to the frequency of the orbiting Scout ships, using authorization codes that they would be particularly likely to recognize.

"Serpent One here."

"And Serpent Two."

"Gentlemen, you have new orders." Tyler knew that these men had been chosen for their obedience, their loyalty to Telford. They had also been chosen for their willingness to bend the rules; their orders had been to destroy any ship that had Steldan aboard it, although his capture, if possible, would have been preferred.

"There will be a ship boosting sometime soon, maybe

in a few days, maybe sooner. You will destroy it, recognizing it by my signal. The transmitted code, as near as possible to the launch, will be 'Iruatnec.' After that, you'll be on your own. There will be money waiting at numbered accounts at the Spaceport bank at Brokin—" He gave the numbers. It occurred to him that if he were Telford, he'd have armed troops waiting instead of money. Telford, for some stupid reason, intended to treat his tools fairly. *Each to his own,* Tyler thought, and after signing off, left the communications cubicle.

His efforts over the next few days to gain custody of Steldan failed. He was not surprised.

Early on the morning of the one hundred and forty-ninth day of the year, Steldan was roused from a fitful sleep by the prison block warder. He was to be taken back to Navy Headquarters at Sopenstil for interrogation. The warder was friendly toward Steldan, as had been most of the officials who'd been in to visit their star prisoner. Despite his throwing the city into a panic with the false explosion threat, he had single-handedly crushed the organized crime and forgery ring that had been strangling the city's commerce.

In one of his many interviews, Steldan had told a C.I.B. interrogator how, and why.

"You'd have cleaned them up, sooner or later."

"Well, yes," the agent had admitted, "but it was likely to be a long war. Of course we tried to infiltrate them, but it always failed. They seemed able to spot our men effortlessly. Further, they assassinated a number of our best men at their homes, where we'd assumed they were safe."

"The criminals had looted the Government files building," Steldan said wearily. The agent nodded.

"And that's why we had no secrets from them. We were lucky, I guess. You came along, with a story that was good enough, and they believed it. And it ruined them."

"They were stupid, mostly. Their organization was poorly pieced together, and they'd made very few plans against their eventual ruin. A standard underworld crime ring, it was divided, shaky, and not built with survival in mind, just quick profit."

"When you broadened the rifts between their branches, were you planning to destroy them?"

"No, it was merely a smokescreen for me to run behind."

"We've spoken with Lieutenant Gray," the agent said, as if Steldan's words had reminded him. "We've made a deal."

Steldan became quite alert.

"From what you've told us about Commander Tyler, and from what we were able to ascertain at that drug bar, I think we'd be smarter not to deal with him. Gray seems far more trustworthy. Further, Gray has the more specific credentials. We've agreed to release you into his custody and drop all local charges. You'll still be liable for Concordat charges, but that's not our responsibility.

"What we've done is guarantee that Tyler doesn't get you." He smiled. "If Tyler takes you from Gray, we'll invoke a court order prohibiting them from taking you off-planet. Then we'll slap fifty or so trifling charges on you, keeping you here."

Steldan shrugged. "It doesn't much matter. I feel like a piece of property, being squabbled over in a small-claims court. I'll be happy as long as Tyler doesn't win."

"He won't. Gray plans to take you off-planet tomorrow, on the morning Courier to Sopenstil. The C.I.B. will provide a small escort to the Spaceport, ostensibly to prevent your escape, but also to keep Tyler at bay. He's made quite a few enemies here, in just a few days."

"He's good at that," Steldan agreed.

Gray arrived shortly thereafter, accompanied by Harcourt and Linde. This time they were admitted in person, no longer separated by the viewscreen. Steldan greeted them, and was introduced to Harcourt. He took her hand gravely, which amused her, and was interrupted by a large and tearful hug from Linde, which Harcourt watched with frank interest.

"Harcourt," Gray suggested quietly, "perhaps we should step outside, and give them a few moments' privacy?"

"Spoilsport," she whispered back, and followed him through the sliding door.

"You won't give up, will you?" Linde asked beseechingly.

"I have the best chance now that I've ever had. I will be heard."

"Part of me wants to follow you, but can't . . . I can't."

"I don't think you could live in my circles, any more than I could live in yours." He disengaged himself from her, and sat on the bed-bench. She sat beside him.

"All my life I've run *toward* things," he said in a voice low and intimate. "A new life; a new idea; a new job. I've only rarely looked back at what I was leaving. Only for these past weeks have I had to run *away,* and I haven't enjoyed it. But it goes beneath that, and beyond it. All my life, I've been running. I'm not sure I'll ever allow myself to stop."

"Will I remain in your memory as . . . a good or an evil thing from this planet?"

"One of the best. You were an enemy, and came to be an ally, and true friend."

"I wanted more."

"I didn't have it in me to give."

"I . . ." She couldn't say it aloud. *I love you still.*

Steldan, not needing to hear the words aloud to know what she meant, said lightly, "I don't know if it helps any, but Gray told me that Harcourt told him . . . that the planetary C.I.B. needs strong people who can shoot straight. How good a shot are you?"

"I hit what I aim for." She turned to him, eyes closed. "Almost always."

After several moments of silence, Harcourt and Gray tapped on the door, then entered. There seemed nothing more to say.

Harcourt, Gray, and Linde left the prison soon afterwards, walking slowly through the bright sunlight and green hedges of the city midmorning, heading for the train station.

"He's such a serious person," Harcourt said to Linde, not caring what Gray thought. "What did you see in him?"

Linde shot Harcourt a glance; had she been a man and said that, she'd have been knocked sprawling. Plainly she hadn't meant anything, and yet . . .

"He was honest, fair, impartial, and always polite." The words poured out as, blushing, she continued. "It wasn't physical attraction, ever. It was . . ." Words failed her. *It was both far more and far less . . .*

"Not *ever?*"

Linde blushed yet further, but managed to say nothing.

"Oh, come along," Harcourt said cheerily. "Lieutenant Gray is taking us both to dinner."

Gray turned to Harcourt, and raised an eyebrow inquisitively; this was the first he'd heard of it. Harcourt wasn't watching, but grasped his hand anyway and led him unresisting to the station. As always, he relented. As Harcourt suggested, the three of them, united only by having once hunted Athalos Steldan, dined together that evening.

In the prison, Steldan slept soundly, and did not dream.

The next day, the block warder gave him to the escort, a well-armed band of three C.I.B. agents. Silently, they took him by air car to the Spaceport, where Gray met him.

"Captain Steldan." Gray, again in full uniform, gray tunic above black pants, black boots gleaming, saluted.

"Lieutenant Gray," Steldan answered in kind, an eyebrow lifted in polite inquiry.

Gray smiled. "Stripped of command, under arrest, doomed for trial . . . All of these, and you're bearing up better than I would be."

Steldan nodded. "The worst is behind me."

Together they turned, as Harcourt pounded across the wind-swept landing field, where they waited in the shadow of the transfer shuttle. She arrived, out of breath.

"A going-away present, Captain Steldan," she puffed. The box she handed him was decoratively wrapped.

With a glance at Gray for permission, which was reluctantly granted, Steldan peeled it, handing the wrapping fragments carefully back to Harcourt. Within the box was a small, silvery cylinder, long and tapering, with control studs of white plastic. Steldan's involuntary bark of laughter left Gray bewildered.

"What is it?"

"A surgical laser," Harcourt explained. "Sequestered and confiscated from the illegal shipment that Steldan had arranged to be pilfered."

Gray snagged it from Steldan's grasp. "Are you mad?" To Steldan: "Are you crazy?" Back to Harcourt: "Are you insane?"

She took it from him and handed it to Steldan. "It hasn't got any charge. It's totally inert."

Gray took it from Steldan. "I can't allow it."

Harcourt took it from Gray. She flipped open the thick end of it, and ejected the power cells. "Here. Without those, it's totally useless as a weapon." She handed it to Steldan, who resealed the end.

Gray reached for it, and changed his mind midway through the gesture. "Why not?" He looked back and forth between them. "Perhaps I'm as insane as you two."

Steldan shrugged. "It is inert . . . and it's not much of a weapon at best."

"It's a keepsake," Harcourt said, holding his hand in hers and closing his fingers over it. "I've had more fun hunting you than doing any other work in my life. You've given me whole volumes of nice tricks." Very seriously: "Good luck, Captain."

He squeezed her hand. "Good luck."

He and Gray boarded the shuttle, which, in a few moments, would lift them to the orbiting Courier. Steldan, during the parting conversation, felt a nervous twitching between his shoulder blades, a manifestation of fear. He imagined Tyler on a balcony on the Spaceport office annex, lining a high-powered rifle on the target that had once eluded him. Would he live?

Nothing happened, and the sense of relief as the hatch closed made him feel almost faint. The outcome was now in the hands of an investigating board on Sopenstil, and it looked like the board would be at least somewhat sympathetic.

Tyler and the pilots of two Serpent class Scoutships had something different in mind. Telford's assassin had indeed been watching from a balcony overlooking the landing field, with his pistol in his hand. At that extreme range, with a good brace for his arm and his familiarity with the weapon, he felt he had a fair chance of putting one of the eight bullets into Steldan's back. But why take chances?

Two Serpents, closing on an unsuspecting Courier, should have no difficulties whatever in making the kill.

He holstered his pistol and watched the shuttle being ferried to the near edge of the boost-grid. There followed a long wait, while traffic-control computers and human operators calculated the flight path. Gray's flight plan involved a seven-jump trip to Sopenstil, aboard the swift Courier.

The shuttle, a smallish in-system spaceship, in shape much like a supersonic airplane, began to rise, pulled upward and inward by differential force from the huge grid. Most of the field's force was focused on the ship, a rising point of light. As the breeze faded, the ship fell upward, then outward, soon to disappear from sight. Gray, Steldan, and some Navy pilot whom Steldan didn't know, would soon dock with their Courier, transfer aboard, and be on their way to Sopenstil. Or so they thought.

Turning, grinning, pushing his blond hair out of his face, Tyler went back into the building. In Gray's now deserted office, he punched a code on the telephone, and asked the switchboard operator for the proper orbital carrier frequency.

Not waiting for an acknowledgment from the Serpents, he said clearly: "Iruatnec," and hung up. Next, he dialed the Spaceport lounge and had Rolle paged.

"Sir?" the quiet aide asked.

"Go get the ship ready. We're going to give our friends some backup." They wouldn't need it, he knew, but it irked him to have matters out of his hands. His small ship had one laser, pin-mounted, and Rolle knew how to use it. They couldn't stand up to a Serpent in a firefight, but the unarmed and unarmored Courier would be another matter. Rolle was a talented enough pilot that it would be a tailing fight, with the enemy's momentum working for him and against them.

Also, he rather wished to witness Steldan's death close-up, even if he couldn't have a hand in it himself. Fifteen minutes later, he and Rolle boosted clear, and sped toward the calculated interception point. Their ship, needle-pointed, stubby-winged, hot and deadly, responded to Rolle's guidance and fled skyward at two and a half gravities. In their acceleration couches, the two waited patiently for the battle to begin.

Space battles are not the swift, darting things that pilots wish they would be. While battles in the atmosphere of a contested planet rage at a pace faster than most pilots can adapt to, fights above the confines of close-orbit space can drag on for long hours, even when only a few ships are involved. If two large fleets meet, the issue may not be decided for days, and the aftermath, with a defeated fleet withdrawing to lick its wounds, can consume another day or two.

Above Chirkun, three small, swift craft endeavored to close with a smaller, swifter ship. Their primary advantage was surprise; an unalerted pilot is often a dead pilot. The young Navy pilot ferrying Steldan and Gray would certainly notice, soon, that three craft out of the dozen or so orbiting were on near-intercept courses. On the other hand, he knew about the Serpents on blockade duty, and believed he could pass them with a coded recognition signal.

Tyler intended that he not be given time to worry about the other ship astern.

Serpent-1, actually, was on the other side of the planet from Leonidas Spaceport when the message "Iruatnec" was relayed to him. His decision was to swing out of his orbit and push for distance, to intercept the target in the event it survived the attack of Serpent-2. He rightfully considered that to be unlikely.

Serpent-2, with this in mind, made a play for time. Approaching the Courier on what looked like a matched-courses trajectory, he radioed his target and asked for identification. Each minute he sped nearer, decreasing the range. Currently, his target accelerated at a gentle one gravity, simplifying his task.

Aboard the Courier *Flippancy*—a ship of the *Trivia* class—Gray lay back in his minuscule cabin, and tried to read. He would share the room (if such a closet could be called a room) with the pilot for the next seven weeks. Steldan, the prisoner, had it worse: for much of the trip he would be confined in the head. Only during the "day" periods, while the pilot sat in the command couch, would Steldan be allowed out.

Both Steldan and Gray thought it ridiculous. Neither of them had flown so much as a spaceflight simulator; the idea of Steldan highjacking the ship was ludicrous. The pilot, however, insisted, and aboard the ship he outranked Gray.

Now, as Gray rested, the pilot buzzed him over the intercom. "Sir?"

Who outranks whom? Gray thought sourly. The pilot couldn't be long out of flight school. "Yes?"

"There's a ship out there, asking for identification."

Gray cursed silently. He thought he'd had Harcourt update the Scoutships. "Put me on. I'll talk to them."

There followed a slight click, and Gray heard the voice of one of the Scouts, asking in a tired voice for authorization.

"Courier *Flippancy,*" Gray responded crisply, "sequence X-114. Lieutenant Ron Gray authorizing."

"Sorry, sir," the voice said, constantly approaching, "but I was ordered to check all departing ships for the fugitive."

"He's not a fugitive. He's been captured. Report to the Portmaster for your new assignment."

"But . . ." The Scout feigned uncertainty. He was still minutes away from the shot he wanted. "According to my orders, I should board you and search . . ." He trailed off. *Mistake,* he thought, and pressed the switch that readied his two missiles. Gray knew what orders had been given, and knew that boarding was specifically not part of the procedure.

Gray caught the error. Uncertain, but with a dire suspicion, he called to the pilot. "Is there a ship following us?"

The pilot glanced at the midsweep scope, and called back, "Yes, sir. And fast."

"Go to maximum speed, and treat the two ships—the Scout and the one following—as if they were combat enemies."

"Yessir." Smoothly, easily, the pilot manipulated the controls, cutting in the acceleration compensators, engaging the computer-evade program, and sliding the acceleration up to the ship's maximum three gravities.

After a few tense minutes, he said to Gray over the intercom, "They're changing course to follow. Looks like they're speeding up."

Then, in the same matter-of-fact voice: "The Scout just loosed a missile. I'll try to evade." He remained calm; combat was unforgiving of those who panicked.

Gray, in the cabin, and Steldan, in the head, were suddenly thrown to the bulkhead as the pilot turned off the artificial gravity acceleration compensators. The danger to the passengers from sudden changes in vector was less important than the energy drain. The pilot now had another half a gravity of thrust to play with. He intended to get all he could from it.

Against the darkness, the stars blotted out in the dazzle of Chirkun's sun, four small ships maneuvered for advantage, and a tiny missile darted. It had its target in its on-board sights; it had the acceleration advantage. Black, trim, already traveling faster than the Courier could ever hope to move, it carried a small, smart warhead at its tip.

Gray had ample time to wonder. *Missile fire?* That was clearly, patently, obviously a violation of the Scout's orders. And yet. . . .

No one, Navy or otherwise, would dare release a nuclear-tipped missile without orders to do so.

Four minutes later, after a brief "Watch yourselves," from the pilot, the Courier changed direction and began an acceleration across the path of the missile. The pilot, hoping that the missile would be unable to turn sharply enough, worked his controls without desperation, without haste. With luck, the missile would spin by, detonating itself uselessly when out of range.

It seemed to work, and the pilot allowed himself the luxury of a brief gasp as the slim weapon passed outside the danger radius. It was a small missile, with a six-gravity engine and limited maneuverability.

Again the pilot applied a transverse thrust, still heading away from the planet, trying to get out of the hampering gravity-well of the world so that he could cut into Jumpspace.

The Scoutship hadn't idled while its missile failed. Under the assumption that it might, the pilot had applied acceleration of his own, trying to line up another shot on the fleeing Courier. "Damned things are built so *fast,*" he muttered, gauging the vectors by his radar screen. He'd have time for his other missile, after which he'd be left behind and out of laser range. "Die, buster," he said softly, and hit the firing stud.

The pilot of the *Flippancy* had expected it, and changed thrust angle once again after the first missile passed by. He desperately wished for an antimissile laser, and, while he was making wishes, for another two or three gravities. Neither was forthcoming.

Gray, recovering from a savage bash received when the ship turned, punched the intercom and asked for a status check.

"The missile is going to hit us. Period." The pilot switched off, and applied even more transverse thrust. Switching back to Gray, he added, "Get into a suit. Both you and your prisoner."

Gray nodded to himself. He released himself from the crash-webbing holding him to the bunk, and crawled to the door. It felt like the pilot was holding the ship steady for the moment. After everyone was suited up, he'd release the hull's air, negating the danger of explosive decompression. Staying low, crawling over the floor-panels under four times his normal weight, Gray moved to release Steldan from the head.

Steldan, however, was already loose, and the panel to the head swung loose. Gray bumped into him, crawling likewise, moving doggedly forward. Bracing himself against the floor that was now a wall, he looked up the heartbreaking cliff-face of the short corridor to the cockpit. He looked back at Gray.

"Combat, right?" His voice was resigned. "I've been trying to call you, but there's no intercom in there."

"How did you get out?"

For an answer, Steldan held up the shining pencil-shape of Harcourt's surgical laser.

Gray frowned. Even now, with a missile closing in at dozens of kilometers per second, all he could do was ask, "How? She said it had no charge?"

"I tapped the power outlet in the head," Steldan smiled. "Now will you get out of my way?"

"Get into a vacuum suit, Steldan. It's our only chance. We're on a collision course with a missile."

Steldan only nodded. "It had to be. We could outrun anything else." He moved across the floor-wall.

"The other way," Gray shouted.

"Nope." Steldan dragged himself to the cabin, wriggled within, and stabbed the intercom button that lay almost beneath him. Breath came to him with difficulty; his arms felt like lead castings of themselves.

"What the hell do you want?" snapped the pilot.

"Switch your navigation radar to wavelength thirty-eight point seven seven meters. Standard waveform."

"Why?"

"Do as he says!" called Gray, who had heard.

The pilot hesitated, having no idea what the useless notion could possibly be in aid of. "Hell. Why not?" he murmured, and reprogrammed the radar with a smooth economy of motion.

As the instrument swept the heavens, tracking the two ships and the missile, its beam contacted the latter. With a silent explosion, the hurtling weapon destroyed itself in flight, growing into a bright flare of thermonuclear energy, and slowly fading.

"What . . ?" asked the pilot, in pleased amazement.

Steldan explained to him, and to Gray, who had already guessed. "After the Battles of Binary, when they changed the self-destruct frequencies on all missiles, the order came through my office."

"That was before they knew that you . . ?" Gray asked.

"That was before *I* knew I had doomed Sienne's fleet! I was given a weaponry order, and I obeyed it. I didn't learn until two years later what I'd done, and right away I reported it to my superior, Commodore Rudolfs." Gray and the pilot listened in attentive fascination. Both of the following ships fell behind the swiftly accelerating messenger ship; the Scout that had sped ahead was not yet within detection range.

"Rudolfs apparently spoke to the wrong people, and got thrown into a high-security prison. They were coming for me when I got a warning and ran."

"Then you're innocent?" Gray asked quietly.

"No. I confirmed the order. By my negligence, I doomed hundreds of thousands of people; I doomed the Sonallans to a bombardment and occupation rather than to just a tactical defeat. I . . ."

"Were you supposed to check the change against enemy radar frequencies?"

Steldan looked down in pain. "It wasn't part of my duties. No. But ordinarily I would have, out of sheer enthusiastic thoroughness." The bitter sarcasm in his voice showed Gray how much Steldan had suffered when he'd learned of his deed. He daily carried the millions of casualties, human and Sonallan, on an overstrained conscience.

"Who gave you the order?"

Steldan met his gaze. "I'll tell the investigating board." Plainly he would say no more.

Gray had no intention of locking Steldan in again, and for the next half hour they spoke quietly of the chase and the capture on Chirkun. As when two players of double-blind chess compare notes and recreate the game, both Steldan and Gray learned much of the other's mind.

The pilot would not relent, and maintained the merciless extra acceleration that pinned them to the floor. Their discussion, and the intellectual fascination of discovering how close they'd been, how many times, kept them from minding.

"Another Scout, sir," the pilot's voice came over the intercom. "Is he an enemy?"

"Assume that he is. What's his course?"

"He's ahead of us, in a nearly matched course. While we dodged the first one, he must have been pushing hard to get here first."

"That settles it, then; he's an enemy."

"What do you want me to do?"

"Stay out of his laser range, and ignore his missiles. They'll blow up in flight as fast as he can launch them, and he only carries two."

"Yes, sir."

"What about the ship that's following us?" Gray asked, knowing the truth now about Commander Tyler.

"He's still back there, and so is the other Scout.

They'd take thirteen minutes to catch up even if we were to lose all power, and that won't happen."

"So we're safe?"

"If the guy in front can't hit us with missiles, we're safe. It's a sure bet he'll get no laser shots."

"Then," Gray said solemnly, "give us our floor fields back." With their gentle return, he slid down the wall to light comfortably on the floor. The fields negated all of his inertial weight save for what he normally would have felt upon a world's surface. The relief was invigorating.

Serpent-1, accelerating at his full two-and-a-half gravities, launched both of his missiles at once. He was amazed to see his target not evading, but merely cruising at three gravities. The speed edge the enemy enjoyed guaranteed that he wouldn't get close enough for a beam shot, but there was no reason to scorn his missiles, was there?

There was. The two missiles burst almost in his face, exploding only microseconds after they'd armed themselves at their minimum safety range. If not for the interlocks, they'd have burst inside his ship, incandescing it and him instantly. The pilot of the *Flippancy* had been playing his radar over the Scout since the two ships came within detection range of each other. The missiles had only waited to be armed before they destroyed themselves.

The pilot of Serpent-1 pushed his ship into a sharp arc to avoid the fireball, pulling him even farther out of range of the escaping Courier. He'd done his best. All he could do now was follow the messenger craft until he, too, was far enough from Chirkun to jump. Since no one had learned how to fight battles in Jumpspace, the Scout pilot had no choice but to jump elsewhere, toward Brokin, where a small, illicit fortune awaited him.

Admiral de la Noue sat, utterly weary, in the smallish conference room on the seventh floor of the Sopenstil Spaceport Naval Office Building. She tried not to listen while one of Cambrai's creatures delivered a haranguing attack on Deacon Anse. Anse sat through it, attentively recording the diatribe in chopped shorthand; Admiral de la Noue watched him across the circle of tables and marveled at his patience. Had the boor now speaking said half as much to her, he'd find himself with more response than he could handle.

Her attention wandered; she wished for a window to gaze through. Bare walls of pale green, a ring of tables, ten hard-bitten Naval officers, and ten sullen deputies of Solme's Court, hemmed her in. She'd been given the job of chairing the investigation over the strictest objections of Cambrai and his more trusted staff members. Apparently, Praesidium orders didn't mean terribly much to them.

Anse and his crew had been softer-spoken although every bit as much opposed. De la Noue felt, with justifiable frustration, that she had been given the post only as a harmless figurehead, unable to guide the committee to any reasonable conclusion. She had been the one with the clean record, the one they had felt would drop the ball and allow the investigation to collapse. Cambrai's men had been worried because she wasn't one of them; Anse and his crew desperately wanted the commission to indict Cambrai and Horst, and perhaps even Telford.

De la Noue was caught in the middle, although she wasn't certain that the Navy faction wasn't going to get what it wanted. It was certain that the committee was disorganized, divided, and deadlocked.

Anse kept promising a first-hand witness to the Battles of Binary, someone who could testify to Cambrai's corruption and to other high-ranking officers' crimes. De la Noue had given up trying to remind him that the committee was called upon to investigate the current situation in the Naval Intelligence Branch's Records Division. Anse, virtually shaking with his frustration, would subside, only to return to the same threadbare theme.

Today, however, he was in a calm, accepting mood that worried de la Noue far more than had his earlier, histrionic overanxiety.

Had he received a communication?

"May I have the floor?" a voice called. De la Noue saw that it was Anse. While she had been ignoring the proceedings—slanderings was perhaps a better word—a messenger had handed Anse a note. Wondering whether her lapse of attention had been noticed, she nodded to him. The other speaker sat down, his sentence unfinished.

"This committee was formed to investigate unspecified crimes in the department of Naval Intelligence Records *and in other, related departments.*"

Brother, thought de la Noue. Was he going to start that again?

"The witness that I've been referring to has arrived." That, from Anse, provoked a stir among the Naval Operations group, who leaned toward one another and conferred. It occurred to de la Noue, for the first time, that she had never met any of these men prior to two years ago. They were all replacements for men who'd died at the First Battle of Binary, or who had retired afterwards to save themselves embarrassment.

It was an open secret that they were all tools of Cambrai and of Telford. How significant was that?

"Gentlemen, Admirals," Anse continued, "I'd like to introduce Athalos Steldan." He sounded as if he were introducing a celebrity, not a fugitive. How had he smuggled the man in?

Into the room Steldan walked, followed by Gray. Both were in uniform, gray tunic above black trousers. Steldan wore his Captain's chip. He strode to the center of the ring of tables, looked about at the assembled committee members, and addressed himself to de la Noue.

"Greetings. I have been hounded across seven weeks of Jumpspace, have hidden in the stench of a foul criminal subculture, and have returned through two attempts on my life, in order to deliver this message: Admiral Telford is a murderer."

The effect of the pronouncement was predictable. From the Navy half of the room came cries of derision and clamors for the slanderer's removal. From the Judiciary half, a stunned silence, with some of the lawyers and clerks looking to Anse and some at Steldan.

De la Noue pounded on the table with the flat of her hand for silence; she wished she'd brought her gavel, a memento of an older day, but still an effective noisemaker. Soon the uproar died away to a muted muttering, with small knots of men on each team trying to guess what Steldan would say next.

"Would you care to expand on that?" asked Anse, usurping for the moment de la Noue's office as chairman. Steldan glanced at him, and looked to de la Noue for permission. At a loss, she nodded; Steldan smiled at her, a little half bow of formality before continuing.

"Before the First Battle of Binary, I was ordered to alter the destruct frequencies of the fleet's missiles. The adjustment was carried out under my supervision, exactly as the orders specified. The operation was classified—for understandable reasons—and elaborate precautions were taken to prevent any knowlege of the new frequency becoming known.

"The new frequency, however, was the same as the Sonallan navigation radar."

There followed another brief uproar, which was cut into by one of Cambrai's men asking very loudly, "Are you admitting your guilt?" Steldan ignored him, and waited for the conversation to fade.

"The change was ordered by Admiral Telford—"

He got no further. Two of the Navy men began shouting at once, so that whatever they had to say was unintelligible. De la Noue considered sending for the guard, although she couldn't be sure that even that would help. Best, she decided, to wait for the noise to die down on its own.

The doors swung open again, and Commander James Tyler burst in. In his hand was his favorite automatic pistol. He threw down on Steldan . . .

And fell, pierced through the lower leg by a snap-shot from Gray. The report echoed, jarring, hollow, in the small room. All sounds came to a halt; the committee members stared in a stunned astonishment too profound for words. Tyler struggled to raise his gun again, until he caught a glimpse of the man who'd shot him. Gray had a steady bead on Tyler, and looked as if only his orders, and not his compassion, had saved the assassin from an instantly fatal wound.

Tyler tossed aside the gun and waited for the medical crew that de la Noue sent for, along with the guard. Only Anse and Steldan retained their composure. Steldan had gone a bit pale, and gazed with distaste at a spot of blood on his jacket; Anse grinned hugely, happy at the outcome and deeply amused by the blank faces of the men on the Navy side of the room.

De la Noue announced an adjournment for twenty

hours, although she knew she would get very little rest during the night, with the interrogation of Tyler and a long discussion with Steldan still before her.

It looked like her committee would have something to report after all.

Admiral Cambrai sat behind his desk and regarded his tormentors with a stony disdain. Facing him were three men from the Judiciary, accompanied by four armed bailiffs. The guards were present more to discourage any abrupt move on Cambrai's part, such as calling in his own Marines, than to threaten him.

"Justicar Solme has agreed not to press the charges against you, provided you hand in your resignation immediately," the first of the investigators said. Cambrai knew him only as one of Anse's men. He appeared disgusted by the lightness of the penalty; he would doubtless have preferred to see Cambrai hanging by his thumbs.

"I intend to stay in this office until carried out," Cambrai replied. It was a bluff, certainly, but he couldn't resist annoying the investigator. The latter glared, his anger building. His orders, however, had been quite clear. He was to give Cambrai every chance to get out quietly, saving the Navy embarrassment.

"The Justicar has more than enough evidence to have you executed," the investigator hissed. "Instead, he offers you this one chance to resign your post and leave the Navy."

"I shall give it all due consideration," Cambrai sneered. "Now please leave." He drew on his pipe, and puffed a large cloud of pungent smoke at the crew. As soon as they left, however, he knew he would begin drafting his resignation. Full retirement pay, with benefits and bonuses, took the sting out of the disgrace. The public would never know, and he could spend the rest of his life as a hero of battle.

Nowhere near as bad as it could have been, he laughed inwardly.

Admiral Telford was to be given no such options. Aboard the *Caerleon,* abandoned now even by his closest advisors, he struggled to find a way out of the rapidly closing trap. The wolves of the past were closing in on him, slavering for the kill.

Apparently, Solme meant to drag him through the mire, to expose the defeat at Binary for what it had indeed been: sabotage. Solme felt, and Telford had to agree, that the public and the fleet would feel better knowing that the Navy hadn't actually lost that battle. That it would undermine the public acclaim the fleet had won during the revenge campaign didn't seem to bother Solme; it would make Vissenne's negotiations with the Sonallans that much easier. Vissenne and Solme wanted the Sonallans pacified by treaty rather than by occupation, freeing those elements of the fleet for other duties.

The Sonallans, Telford knew, if released from their captivity, would rearm, and some day his successor would have to put them down again. The fleet he'd murdered—he had to admit that murder was the correct word—was nothing compared to the battle losses that would follow a lengthy campaign.

And, damn it, he knew he'd done a better job than that soft clod Sienne, may he rot! The fleet now had a higher efficiency rating than it had shown for years. Stockpiles were up; readiness was unparalleled. Vissenne would deal with aliens that were far too humanlike to trust. The Sonallans were dangerous, scheming, warlike aggressors.

Like a slap in the face, the thought came to Telford: *It takes one to know one.*

But what I've done, I've done for lasting peace. That region would have been under the enemy's threat for centuries, had I not crushed it. He'd purchased lasting security; wasn't that worth the lives of the men who'd trusted him? Wasn't the safety of billions more vital than the lives of thousands? Wasn't it?

It didn't matter. Solme and Vissenne had done their jobs, uncovering what he'd done. They were willing to undo two years of hard work, seeing his last act only as a calculated, treacherous grab for power.

He was virtually a prisoner aboard his ship. Welch, the ship's Captain, had been ordered to disregard any instructions Telford might give him, and to keep the Grand Admiral aboard. Any general or fleet orders he tried to issue would be intercepted or filtered by Solme's agents. And Anse, the squat lawyer, the muscular little clerk, was due to arrive, to interview him in Solme's name, inside an hour.

Was there a possibility of some of his loyal staff officers putting together a rescue? Perhaps coupled with some propaganda campaign to put a different light on things?

More likely the wretches were lying low, hoping to retain their posts despite the avalanche of evidence descending upon them.

Think, damn it! How can I save things?

And then it was too late. Into his office stalked Anse, de la Noue, and Steldan. He looked up, and wondered how he appeared to them.

"Admiral Telford," Anse intoned by way of a greeting. After introducing Steldan, whom Telford had never met, and de la Noue, Anse settled into one of the Grand Admiral's soft chairs, motioning the others to do likewise. It was Anse's moment, and not even Telford could blame him for the joy he took in it.

A long silence slipped by, during which Steldan and Telford studied each other. Each was impressed with the other's bearing; each felt a measure of respect behind his enmity.

"Did you do it?" de la Noue asked. "Did you murder Sienne's fleet?" Telford was amused by her directness.

"What do you plan to do with me?" he returned, avoiding her question.

"Solme wants you exposed. He wants everything out in the open. The sabotage, the coverup, everything. He wants you tried, convicted, and executed, all in public."

"He's been listening to that fool Vissenne," Telford stated quietly. "Vissenne wants the Navy crippled, although I've never known why."

Anse spoke, softly, sardonically. "Grand Admiral Telford, what would be *your* recommendation? How do *you* propose we deal with you? What would *you* like us to do?"

Telford refused to rise to the bait. "Do what you must."

"Indeed." Anse turned to de la Noue. "Well, then, what would you have us do with him?"

She frowned. "Public exposure would hurt the Navy,

it's true . . . Nevertheless, the truth must be known. Get it into the daylight." She had the strength to meet Telford's gaze.

"And Captain Steldan. Telford used you, then he tried to have you killed. What would *you* like to see happen to him?" Anse's grin was huge.

"Charge him with a lesser offense—abuse of power, perhaps—to which he will plead guilty. Accept his resignation. Let him go."

"Why in hell—" Anse sputtered, his grin stricken from his face. More calmly he began again. "He tried to kill you, and you're supporting him? Why? If what you suggest happens, he'll be retired with only the most ritual penalties . . . It's unthinkable!"

"Anse, have you taken a good look at the Concordat lately? Have you looked beyond your closed concerns at the Justice Branch, and seen what's happening?" Steldan turned to face Anse and de la Noue. "The cycle is turning. We're in a twilight phase, an autumn. The lessons that we learned in The Revolution are at last being forgotten. History has shown us the way to survive: don't make waves.

"The planets are emphasizing their independence, while the Praesidium fragments. If you don't want one member to become all-powerful, you can't afford to drag one down. If Telford is disgraced, who'd take over the Navy? Would the military retain its Praesidium seat? Could the Praesidium survive with only five members?

"Telford must go; there's no debate on that." He turned and faced the Grand Admiral. "But I oppose tearing the Navy apart because of it."

"I disagree completely," de la Noue said firmly. "It sets a bad precedent." Telford looked at her as if he'd expected nothing less. Steldan showed some surprise. Anse appeared thoughtful, almost undecided.

"Criminals must be punished," she continued, "and the Concordat is hardly so frail as to crumble when this . . . murderer is removed.

"Are you claiming that the Sector governments are becoming satrapies? I don't think they are. I feel that the planets aren't independent enough.

"A decline? We're stronger than we've ever been before, and not just in our military."

"I hope you're right," Anse muttered.

"We'll be able to see," Steldan said quietly. "Because if I'm correct, the next forty years will see a cycle of revolutions, some of them armed, and some of them purely ideological. If I'm right—and I dare not believe otherwise—the revolutions will begin soon. One year? Two years? Will it be separatism? Monarchism? Supernaturalism?

"I won't apologize. I'm afraid."

Anse blinked.

De la Noue shook her head, disagreeing and more than disagreeing. "I'm certain that you're wrong." A smile came to her. "I think that in this case, you'd be happiest if that was so. I won't despair. Even if you're right, we can still survive. We've had troubled periods in our history before now, and we've come through them. Of course, it's true that the years following a war are the most dangerous, domestically. Can't you see?" She smiled, bravely. " 'We Strive; We Will Secure Us; We Shall Endure.' "

Anse threw Steldan a glance. Steldan nodded.

Telford watched, and his face was quietly thoughtful.

"One of the best ways to survive a twilight phase," Steldan said at last, "is to install a strong, clean leader, behind whom the populace can rally."

"And this swamp has innocence enough for any job," Anse agreed. "That's settled, then. Solme will agree. I'll see to it. I, too, have read the works theorizing the cycles of civilization, and find them compelling. I've been too engrossed in the hunt to think this far beyond it."

"What do we do with Telford?" Steldan asked.

"What are you maniacs talking about? What's settled?" De la Noue looked at them in frustration.

"Well," Anse began cautiously, "with Telford and Cambrai gone, command would logically devolve onto you . . ."

"Giving me the job won't change my mind. And in any case, Telford's announced successor is Admiral Horst."

"The Praesidium would never accept him," Anse said sourly. "They will accept you."

"Do you think I care about that? I won't let the crime

go unpunished. That is all that matters here; that's my sole duty now."

Telford spoke then, in a voice so low that he could barely be heard. "Take the job. I'll resign in your favor. Do you think that the realities of the situation can take into account whether or not you care?"

De la Noue glared at him. "You've read about cycles also? Was it for the common good of the Concordat that you destroyed that fleet?"

"Yes . . . No . . . Partly it was. Sienne couldn't handle it. I knew I could do a better job. What I did needed doing."

De la Noue refused to discuss it further. It didn't matter. With his voting block on the investigating committee, and with the Navy block abstaining according to Telford's request, the final recommendation was passed as Anse dictated. Admiral de la Noue left the room angrily, dissatisfied with the results. That didn't matter either.

Two days later, Justicar Solme received Telford's resignation, along with the recommendation that Admiral de la Noue be accepted as the new Secretary. Telford quietly yet officially nominated her as his successor. Within the week, a final vote had been formally taken, and no one had doubted the outcome.

At Grand Admiral de la Noue's inauguration party, where she, to her disgust, was presented to the Concordat ruling elite as an equal, Steldan was reunited with his superior, Commodore Rudolfs.

"Just imprisonment." He gestured expansively to Steldan. "Nothing worse. I most missed cigars." Judging from the large pocketful he carried with him, it was obvious that he intended some catching up. Becoming serious for a moment, he gripped Steldan's elbow and muttered, "Thanks for getting me out. Who knows what they'd have eventually decided to do?" He released Steldan and grinned sourly. "But no thanks for getting me imprisoned in the first place. Have a cigar. Does de la Noue smoke? I haven't had time to purchase a nicer gift . . ." He moved off into the louder part of the party, puffing furiously on one cigar and lighting another. Steldan tucked the gift cigar back into Rudolfs' briefcase, which he'd left by his chair.

Anse came in soon after, seeing Steldan in the quiet lounge, and looking about to see that they were alone. He sat, and leaned close. "Gray sends his regards. He couldn't attend, he said, because he was too busy watching Tyler. The rascal almost escaped twice, and Gray thought he'd best watch him himself."

"What's to happen with Gray?"

"With the restructuring of the Intelligence Branch, he'll likely be promoted fairly rapidly. He sent you this, as a keepsake." He opened his briefcase, and gave Steldan a peek within. Between sheafs of papers, Tyler's pistol snuggled. "I'll hold on to it and give it to you after the party."

A caterer wandered into the room and politely inquired whether either of them wished for refreshments. Neither did.

Once again alone with Steldan, Anse gestured briefly toward the main ballroom. "She's inexperienced. Vissenne sees that as an advantage. Solme and Parke liked her record, and Wallace and Redmond didn't care one way or the other, so they approved her." He sighed heavily. The music and lights seemed dimmed in the lounge.

"Things will get worse before they get better," Anse said at last. "A cliché, but unfortunately a true one. By the time she finds herself foremost among the Praesidium members, she'll have the experience as well as the power. We've made the best decision available."

"And Telford?"

"He's going home to Jewell, on a reduced pension and a suspended sentence. I expect he'll make himself known in Sector-level decision-making—and the Line Worlds is the place that can best use him. The Concordat, for now at least, is free of him." He handed an envelope to Steldan. "Your new assignment. Rudolfs is retiring also, and they've combined your office with his. Grand Admiral de la Noue, on the other hand, put aside our recommendation that you be promoted to Commodore."

"Oh, just as well. A Captain's rank-chips always looked fancier than a Commodore's anyway."

Together they turned and looked toward the brighter

ballroom where conversation and music pulsed and varied.

"Do you think she'll ever forgive us?"

"I doubt it."

In the ballroom, in a new, freshly pressed uniform of bright red, trimmed with crisp white, the new Grand Admiral was already making enemies, and allies, and commitments.